Pointers for playing Mary in a nativity pageant:

1. Think what it would be like if an angel came down and spoke to you. Yikes! Even being queen of the Rose Parade doesn't prepare you for that one.
2. Get into the mindset of having the biggest secret in the world. That's me. I have a secret that I should have told my friends years ago.
3. Work on having inner beauty. Which isn't easy when all your life people have been telling you you're beautiful—on the outside.
4. Pray. Faith is something I lacked for a long time, but now that I'm praying again, I find it helps me with every aspect of my life.

Books by Janet Tronstad

Love Inspired

**An Angel for Dry Creek* #81
**A Gentleman for Dry Creek* #110
**A Bride for Dry Creek* #138
**A Rich Man for Dry Creek* #176
**A Hero for Dry Creek* #228
**A Baby for Dry Creek* #240
**A Dry Creek Christmas* #276
**Sugar Plums for Dry Creek* #329
**At Home in Dry Creek* #371
***The Sisterhood of the Dropped Stitches* #385
**Shepherds Abiding in Dry Creek* #421
***A Dropped Stitches Christmas* #423

*Dry Creek
**The Sisterhood of the Dropped Stitches

JANET TRONSTAD

grew up on a small farm in central Montana. One of her favorite things to do was to visit her grandfather's bookshelves, where he had a large collection of Zane Grey novels. She's always loved a good story.

Today, Janet lives in Pasadena, California, where she is a full-time writer. In addition to writing novels, she researches and writes nonfiction magazine articles.

A Dropped Stitches Christmas

Janet Tronstad

Published by Steeple Hill Books™

STEEPLE HILL BOOKS

ISBN-13: 978-0-373-87459-0
ISBN-10: 0-373-87459-6

A DROPPED STITCHES CHRISTMAS

This edition published by arrangement with Steeple Hill Books.

www.SteepleHill.com

Printed in U.S.A.

For with God nothing shall be impossible.
—*Luke* 1:37

I dedicate this book to my friend and neighbor
N. Courtney White, with thanks for her
encouragement and positive attitude.

Scripture

"Behold, a virgin shall be with child, and shall bring forth a son, and they shall call his name Emmanuel, which being interpreted is, God with us."

—*Matthew* 1:23

Chapter One

"I have no dress except the one I wear every day. If you are going to be kind enough to give me one (a wedding dress), please let it be practical and dark so that I can put it on afterwards to go to the laboratory."

—*Marie Curie*

It was a good thing Marie Curie was dead or her ears would have been ringing from all of the indignant protests when Rebecca read this quote to us years ago. The four of us—Marilee Davidson, Rebecca (Becca) Snyder, Lizabett MacDonald and me, Carly Winston—were sitting in a small room at the hospital with Rose, our counselor. Rose is the one who asked us to bring the quotes. It was almost Christmas and we were having our second meeting of the Sisterhood of the Dropped Stitches. Rose had been looking for a more cheerful place for us to meet, but we were content in that hospital room with its bad lighting, plastic chairs and the smell we could only hope was disinfectant. There weren't many regular places where we felt we belonged, not with our balding heads and our talk of chemo. That's why Becca brought us this quote. She said we were afraid to attract any attention to ourselves, just like Marie Curie had been on her wedding day.

I'm sure Becca thought that I would be completely horrified that any woman would ask for such a go-nowhere wedding dress. But she was wrong. I might have been the only one sitting in that hospital room who had actually given the beauty queen wave to a crowd of people instead of just to her own mirror, but I absolutely knew there was more to life than clothes.

Madame Curie's compelling research, like our cancer, stripped away most of the natural pleasantness of life until just one thing remained. For her that one thing was the cure; for us it was the disease. At times like that, pretty clothes weren't worth a moment's thought.

I'm twenty-four, by the way, and I'm the second oldest member of the Sisterhood of the Dropped Stitches. On the surface, we're a knitting group. In reality, we started to meet as teenage cancer patients and that, more than the endless skeins of yarn, is what has kept us together for more than six years now.

Being in the Sisterhood gave us great courage,

and we're trying to use that courage to take back our lives. We all know cancer put us a step or two behind most people our age. But what the others in the Sisterhood don't know, and I'm just starting to realize, is that I'm not just a step or two behind; I'm walking backward down a whole different street. I need courage more than anyone else in the Sisterhood, because I haven't been open with anyone.

I should have told the Sisterhood my family secret years ago. But secrets can be seductive things. A small secret, and it was a small secret at first, doesn't seem worth telling. Then it becomes a big secret and becomes too hard to tell. Now I wonder what they will think of me if they know I'm not the person they think I am.

It was the end of November when the Sisterhood started to meet that first year. I remember when we introduced ourselves, and I said I lived in San Marino. If you know the area, you know it's *very* upscale. It takes lots of money to live there and, when I said I did, the others assumed I had it made with a trust fund and a servant or two. Which was cool, I let them think that. I didn't tell them that I only lived there as an unwelcome guest, along with my parents, in my uncle's house.

My uncle is rich, but I'm blue-collar poor.

My mother is ashamed that her brother is supporting us, and I never advertise the fact myself. None of my friends know that my parents and I are one careless word away from being homeless and have been for years now. My uncle is known for his temper, and I used to keep a small suitcase packed just in case someone said the wrong thing.

Early on, my mother encouraged me to look like I belonged in San Marino. She probably thought my uncle might like having us around if we looked like the neighbors. Back then I saw it as camouflage. So I did the hair and the dress and the attitude. It seemed to make sense at the time, but I'm beginning to realize I've pretended so long that I don't know who I am anymore.

I need to tell the rest of the Sisterhood about me, but I can't bring myself to do it just yet. I didn't realize what years of living a little lie would do. I guess I never expected the Sisterhood to become so important to me. Or that the things we said in those early meetings would have any significance beyond those days.

Frankly, I never really thought we'd stay together long enough to make it out of that hospital room. And we might not have except, a couple of weeks after we started meeting, Marilee's uncle offered us the use of the back room at his diner in old-town Pasadena, California. He'd stored a damaged pool table in the room before he cleared it out and added French doors so we could see out into the main dining area. I know Rose thought we'd start talking to each other more when we had a nice room like that, and it made her even more determined to keep us together.

In those days, we had no words for anyone. We were afraid for our lives. Marilee had breast cancer. I had Hodgkin's disease. Becca had a bone tumor. Lizabett had a tumor in the muscle of her leg.

Looking back, I don't think any of us wanted to stay together. But we didn't have the energy to tell Rose so we just kept on meeting and meeting. Through the chemo, through the radiation, through the wigs. Through that Christmas and the next one. By the time we each had our five-year clearance from cancer, we had grown so tight nothing could pry us apart.

It's the story of this struggle back to being normal that Marilee wants to tell in our journal. She started writing it several months ago, saying we need to show the world that our cancer didn't drain the very life out of us; that we kept our spirit and we survived.

The journal is her little victory dance on behalf of us all and her joy in it warms me.

You'd like Marilee. She's a cross between a Girl Scout leader and the girl next door. If she sees anyone in pain, she's right there with a Band-Aid or an aspirin or a *kidney.* Seriously, she's always looking out for the other guy—unless, of course, she's asking someone, like me, to write in the journal. Then she's Attila the Hun on a rampage.

I might approve of the journal, but I don't want to write in it. Now that I'm more aware of my secrets, I'm afraid they will seep out onto the pages without my knowing it, even though we all clip pages back or tape them together when we want them to be private.

When Marilee shoved the journal into my hands a little while ago, I was trapped. I like Marilee too much to disappoint her. Besides, she had already given me the equivalent of a kidney when she gave me her forever boyfriend. He's the man she had fantasized about through all the years when she had cancer and he's come back to work for a couple of weeks at her uncle's diner. So what did she do when she found this out? She decided I should date him instead of her.

Which is why I couldn't say no to writing in the journal. Talk about guilt. Marilee gave up her dream for me. I'd rather disappoint my own mother than cause any grief to Marilee. So, of course, I politely told the guy "no, thank you" when he asked me out and tried to give him back to Marilee.

I've been trying for several months now, but she won't take him back.

We're sitting in a Sisterhood meeting right now and talking about the guy. We call him "the grill guy" because Marilee called him that for years. His name is Randy Parker and he's going to be working the grill at The Pews for the next two weeks. Marilee's uncle is finally going on vacation and Randy is filling in for him. It took Marilee's uncle, Lou, longer than anyone thought it would to organize everything, but he is flying to Venice, Italy tomorrow and Randy will be here at The Pews several hours every day working the grill. I think they are swapping time and that Randy will go on vacation next and Uncle Lou will help manage Randy's diner for him when he's gone.

"If you're both so *busy,* I could date him," Becca finally says after Marilee and I spend ten minutes telling each other why we are too involved with other things to go on a date with Randy.

"That's fine with me. I have Quinn," Marilee says. She is blushing and knitting a blue scarf for the new man in her life. Quinn is a firefighter that she met a few months ago. I think the scarf is her Christmas present to him, because when I offered her some red silk yarn that makes those new sparkly scarves, she said the yarn had to be blue to match the person's eyes.

"Besides, Randy is really more your type," Marilee says as she looks over at me.

I freeze. "What do you mean?"

Marilee shrugs. "He's just got that San Marino look."

Boom. Who knew my secret would lead to this? "There is no San Marino look."

"Plea-ea-se," Marilee says as she rolls her eyes.

"Even if there were such a look, I wouldn't need a San Marino–look guy. I'm not as San Marino as you think."

Marilee smiles. "You may as well date him. I'm happy with Quinn."

I must admit that Quinn is nice, but Marilee hasn't been dreaming about him for the past six years. Besides, Marilee would give me her last saltine cracker if we were stranded on a desert island and there wasn't another cracker in sight and she was feeling queasy, (Marilee always had saltine crackers with her to help settle her nausea when she was taking chemo). Not only would she give me the last cracker, she would insist that I needed it more than she did. That's Marilee.

I wonder if Randy is a little like that cracker and that she thinks I need him more than she does so she's being noble.

Not knowing what else to do, I am writing in the journal. Between the cracker theory and the San Marino–look comments, I'm beginning to realize that my lack of candor about my family might be affecting us all. If Marilee is thinking I should date Randy because he *looks* San Marino and I *am* San Marino, then we have a problem.

I might live in San Marino, but I don't belong there.

I can't just blurt out that I've let them believe a lie, however. Besides, if I say I'm really poor, Marilee might decide I need the cracker even more. No, now's not the time to tell everyone.

Maybe if I write for a while something will come to me. I don't know what to do but to write about what's happening now, though, so that's what I've been doing.

We're in The Pews, of course, at our table in the

back room. It's almost Christmas again and last week we hung red garland from the ceiling fan and stood a plastic snowman on the bookshelf. December in Pasadena is a little cold, so we have the heat turned on and the flow of the warm air moves the garland slightly. Becca is looking up from the cap she is knitting to see if anyone has any response to her halfhearted offer to date Randy. Becca is going to force us to deal with this issue. Not that I should be surprised. She is the most forthright person I know and she expects that same honesty from each of us.

When I first met Becca, she was sixteen and everything about her, from her short black hair to her wiry frame, made her look like a teenage activist. I wasn't surprised that she was fiery. I was a little unnerved by her directness, though, and she hasn't mellowed over the years. Becca believes that if a person has a sliver, someone needs to yank it out whether the person wants it to be pulled or not. I'm more the kind of person who likes to coax my slivers out with a little ointment and maybe some soft pressure.

I suppose that's obvious because of my reluctance to blurt out that I've been an imposter. I try not to show Becca any slivers in my life until I've taken care of them myself. Ironically, she has no idea how many slivers I have in my life right about now. I'm not even sure I do.

Our counselor, Rose, is not here tonight, so the

only other person sitting here knitting is Lizabett. She's pretending not to listen to the conversation Marilee and I are having because Quinn is her older brother and she is trying to be neutral. I can see she's having a hard time keeping her opinion inside, however, and that's good for Lizabett. She was fifteen when we started to meet so she's the youngest of the Sisterhood and the most shy. Everyone tells her she needs to learn to speak her mind.

I decide to give Lizabett some hope.

"You don't have to stop dating Quinn to date Randy." I say the words to Marilee, but I intend them for Lizabett. "You're not exclusive with anyone. It would just be a date. You don't have to choose between the two guys. There's no hurry. We've got time."

At those last words, all four of us look up and grin at each other. We forget about journals and guys and what season it is. We have time. Those words are sweet to four people who once thought time was the one thing they didn't have.

"Praise God," Marilee says.

I grunt in what I hope is an acceptably nonjudgmental way. It is Christmas, after all, so I should expect people to talk about God. Even those people ringing the bells for donations say something about God when a person puts in some money.

When I think of God, I always think of my uncle frowning as he reads the *Wall Street Journal.* My uncle is very well informed and he does his duty, but he doesn't like people. Frankly, it makes me nervous to picture someone like that in charge of the world. We already have enough problems.

Marilee found God about the same time she decided Quinn was the love of her life, and I don't trust fast changes like that. Even with my uncle, it takes some time before he shows his true self to people. I wish Marilee had waited a bit longer to make her decisions about God and Quinn. She had never been cozy with God before she met Quinn and she'd dreamt about Randy a lot longer than she'd dreamt about Quinn.

Randy worked the grill for Marilee's uncle one summer while he was in college. That was the summer Marilee got her diagnosis. All we heard in the Sisterhood was "the grill guy this" and "the grill guy that." Well—hello, Marilee. The grill guy is finally back. Merry Christmas.

If I've learned anything in life, it is to take things slow. No one needs to fall in love overnight and no one needs to start talking about God all of a sudden. God's been around forever so He can wait a bit. I certainly have no intention of joining the hallelujah choir alongside Marilee anytime soon, not even if it is the season.

Fortunately, Marilee hasn't gone all holy on us even though she has started going to church and saying things like she just said.

"It's good to be alive," Becca says with satisfaction.

We all nod. I don't think it's by chance that we

all glance up and look through the French doors. For so many Christmases, the people on the other side of those doors seemed to have golden lives. They'd sit there laughing with their friends while we were back here worrying about staying alive. That first Christmas, we wouldn't let Uncle Lou put decorations in our room and then we sat here jealous when we looked through the windows and saw the holiday fantasy he'd created on the other side.

Not that anyone could blame us. Who could not notice the difference when it was Christmas? We were like orphans in some Charles Dickens book; everyone else seemed happier. Now, though, we're on equal footing with the people on the other side of the French doors and it is good to be alive. This year we even decorated. I think I might even bring in more red garland for our room and maybe some gold glittery stuff.

"Besides, I already went on a date with Randy," Marilee says after a moment has passed. Her eyes turn from the crowd out front and meet mine. "Remember? He and I went out for coffee that night at the place in DeLacey Alley."

Marilee calls DeLacey an alley even though it's an avenue that just looks like an alley. Some of the hottest places in old town are in the alleys and the side streets. The main street, Colorado Boulevard, has these turn-of-the-century stone buildings that have been restored and filled with exclusive stores and really good restaurants. The alleys have the same style, but they are quieter, which makes them seem a little more European. And, with the Victorian swags on their signs this time of year, they look elegant.

"That wasn't a date," I say. "You and Randy weren't even gone for half an hour. That's barely a decent work break."

Not that either of them were working that night so they didn't even have that excuse for their short time together.

I suppose I shouldn't keep pressing Marilee on this. It's just that I have to be absolutely certain that she has no feelings for Randy and I think a cup of coffee isn't really a good enough test after six years of daydreams.

"But she met her dating goal," Becca says with a shrug. She's the one who always keeps us on track with goals and, I must admit, going on three dates had been Marilee's goal just like getting a cat had been my goal. Dancing in a ballet had been Lizabett's goal and she was in a community Swan Lake performance several months ago. Becca met her goal and she's currently serving an internship with a judge before she goes to law school next year.

"Besides, Randy can't take his eyes off of you," Marilee says to me with a smile. "You were all he and I talked about when we had our coffee."

I was afraid of that. "Just because he talked about me, it doesn't mean anything. You know how guys are."

"How's that?" Becca says with a frown. She

looks up from the turquoise cap she's knitting for a Hanukkah gift.

I know Becca would probably let the subject drop if I gave her a look that asked her to back off. But these are the best friends I've ever had in my life. If I can't say it to them, I can't say it to anyone.

"Well." I take a deep breath. "With me, I've noticed that guys might want to date me, but they don't want to get to know me." I say the words quickly before I lose my nerve. "Not really."

Everyone looks at me in astonishment.

"Of course guys want to get to know you," Becca says. "You're gorgeous."

I grunt.

"And you're nice, too," Lizabett adds.

"They don't care. I could be the wicked witch of never-never land. They don't care *who* I am. They see a blond, blue-eyed woman with a San Marino address and the right clothes and they think their friends will be jealous of them if they show up with me, so they do."

I hadn't quite realized how it was with guys and me until I got cancer. Guys still wanted to take me out and around, but they'd just as soon I smiled and kept my mouth shut when we were with other people. I knew cancer was a downer, but that was my life then. I was tired of having to pretend my charmed life was as perfect as it looked, so I gave up on dating.

"Well, Randy's not like that," Marilee says.

I'm not surprised she's defending him. She had those six years.

"Maybe not." But I say it because I don't want Marilee to think any less of her dream man.

"Randy was even worried about your *cat,*" Becca adds. "I don't think most guys would rig up that trap with the tuna and—"

I can tell the exact second when Becca realizes I had asked Randy not to trap my runaway cat. I wanted to wait for my Marie to come out of the tree and back into the house all on her own. Everyone, even a cat, should be free to choose where they live.

"Randy wasn't patient enough," I say. "That's never a good sign in a man."

"I think he likes *you* though," Marilee says. "He's not just trying to impress his friends."

"He doesn't have any friends out here, anyway," Becca adds. "I mean, I'm sure he has tons of friends down in West Hollywood by his diner, but you don't need to worry that he's planning to run into them here in Pasadena."

Randy owns this sports diner in West Hollywood and enough of the professional athletes in L.A. hang out there to make it very successful.

"Besides," Marilee says, "you are a beautiful woman so a guy *is* getting to know you when he thinks that."

I shake my head and start pointing to my teeth. "Braces."

I point at my nose. "Nose job."

I point at my hair. "Dark roots, blond highlights."

I touch my cheekbones. "Freckles bleached away."

I turn to look at everyone. "I don't even know what I would look like if my mother wasn't so determined to see me look like this."

I don't need to look in anyone else's eyes to know I have a tear in my own. Which is why I'm not comfortable with letting my emotions out. They come out messy, especially around the holidays. I'm not sure I'm ready to give up more secrets.

After a moment, Becca straightens her shoulders. "If it would make you feel better, you can go back to your natural hair color. You don't need to be your mother's Barbie doll."

"I know," I say. "But after all this time, it seems like I should be okay with myself no matter how I look. It's the inside that counts anyway."

Maybe it's no coincidence that the discussion we had years ago about Marie Curie's dress has been swirling around in my mind lately. We have to be about more than how we look or what address we have. Marie knew that. I knew that when I had cancer. I don't know why it's starting to bother me now.

"Remember Marie Curie's wedding dress?" I ask the others. They haven't seen what I was writing earlier, but they all nod. We talked about that dress for weeks. "Maybe the problem with me isn't how I look, but that I need to find something to do that makes me not care about how I look."

Becca nods. "I always thought your goal was too easy. I should have made you pick something besides getting a cat."

"But it's a Maine coon cat. I had to go to Seattle to get her. Besides, I love my Marie."

I named my cat after Marie Antoinette but she could be named for Marie Curie, too.

"But your cat's not a challenge. You need a deeper goal, something you're afraid to reach for. With Marilee it was dating, but for you it should be—"

"The movies," Lizabett almost shouts she's so excited. "Carly should be in the movies."

Lizabett has been quietly knitting so the rest of us are a bit startled when she makes her proclamation. Her face is flushed and she's got a big smile. She's always wanted me to be in the movies.

Lizabett's shout causes a couple of people from the outside room to look back at us through the glass panes in the French doors. I can see they're curious and it strikes me that, for as long as the Sisterhood has been meeting here, not many people out here have glanced back at us and wondered who we are. Uncle Lou keeps the room just for us, so the people must know we're not customers like they are. It's odd to realize we've been invisible to them all that time when we were so very jealous of them.

It's a new experience to be staring at the people on the other side of the doors and watching them stare back at us.

"I don't know that people find themselves in the

movies," Marilee says as she deliberately turns her head so she's not looking at the people looking at us.

"But Carly has always wanted to be an actress," Lizabett says. She seems to be oblivious to anyone looking through the glass panes at us. "She could be as good as Meryl Streep. Better maybe."

"It's not that easy to be an actress," I add just so we keep the conversation going. I want the people on the other side of the door to know we have things to talk about, too. "No one is discovered just sitting in a drugstore in Hollywood anymore."

"No, we will need a plan to make it all happen," Becca says and I can hear the satisfaction in her voice as she sets down the cap she's knitting. Becca loves goals and plans. I bet she'll become a judge some day and rule the world. I'd vote for her. Or obey her. Whatever it is one does for a judge.

"Write this down," Lizabett says as she points to the journal I have sitting in front of me. Of course, they would all want me to write down my acting fantasy so that the whole world knows that I am setting a goal that is so far-fetched that I'm almost certain to fail. I already know there's no Santa Claus coming down anyone's chimney at Christmas. Do I have to add my name to the list of no-shows?

The only good thing is that Marilee is smiling at me now. If I can't give her her dream man back, at least I can keep everyone amused as we work on making me a star. There will be time later to talk about houses and uncles and who owns what.

I turn the page of the journal and write, "Carly's Aim for Stardom Begins."

"See?" I show the others. "It's down there in black and white."

"Put the date," Lizabett adds.

I add December 9 and, with that, I close the journal.

I'm going to leave the journal here tonight. This journal comes from all of us and I'm sure someone will be anxious to write in it tomorrow and tell everything that I am doing wrong in taking the first step toward my goal. But at least, if the Sisterhood is urging me to become a star, they won't be asking me why I won't go out with Randy Parker.

Which is good because I don't really know why I don't want to go out with him. I'm beginning to think Marilee is happy with her Quinn. Maybe it's not about her feeling sorry for me and giving me the cracker or even about the San Marino look. Maybe worrying about her is just an excuse for me not to date Randy. To tell you the truth, I'm a little nervous about dating him. What if Becca is right and he does want to get to know me?

When I was thinking about the Marie Curie dress earlier, I thought about how little a dress tells us about someone. When I first got cancer, I felt like clothes were a costume I could use to hide the real me. I could put on lipstick and a new DKNY tank top and I looked like every other eighteen-year-old heading off to San Marino High. Long, blond hair bouncing along behind me. A winter tan that was half salon and half leftover beach on my face. No one would ever know by looking at me that inside I was wasting away from Hodgkin's disease.

By now, of course, everybody knows about the Hodgkin's, but I'm still not comfortable telling people things about myself. I'm not sure how I'd go about telling Randy about me, that's for sure. He already knows about the cancer and I can bluff my way through talking about becoming a movie star.

But what about my family?

As you know, even the Sisterhood doesn't know about my crazy family. That's the problem with dating Randy. He'd expect to meet my parents. Worse than that, my mother might expect to meet him.

Yikes.

And I'm not even worried about who owns the house. My mother is funny about me and dating. Sometimes I think she measures her happiness by the number of dates I have. Which I know can't be good. It certainly makes me feel trapped, like I should go out with a guy whether I want to or not. So, mostly I just say no to any guy who asks me out. Which, of course, doesn't make my mother happy and we start the cycle all over again.

Truthfully, it might be easier to become an actress like Meryl Streep than to have a normal dating relationship in my family. I'm not going to put that down in the journal, though. There aren't enough staples left in the stapler to keep that page secure.

Chapter Two

"I'm not funny. What I am is brave."
"I regret the passing of the studio system. I was very appreciative of it because I had no talent."
—*Lucille Ball*

Lizabett brought these quotes to us when she was completely bald. She used to play old I Love Lucy *reruns and laugh and laugh. She even got a bandana and wore it tied over her head like Lucy used to do when she was doing housework. Lizabett seldom wore a wig. She used scarves or caps or turbans instead. I think Lucy inspired her to be brave. When Lizabett's hair grew back, it came back with a tinge of red in it. We all said it was because of all the Lucy shows she'd watched.*

I think Lizabett is still watching those Lucille Ball shows. That's the only reason I can think of for her to be standing here this morning in The Pews, telling me I've got what it takes to become an actress.

We took the bus down Colorado together and arrived a few minutes ago. She has a cup of herbal tea in front of her and I have a cup of black coffee in front of me.

We're both leaning on the mahogany counter that runs along the left side of the diner. Uncle Lou (we all call him Uncle Lou even though he's Marilee's uncle) keeps that counter so polished a person can almost see their reflection. I can actually see more than that. If I focus on the wood at the end of the counter, I can look into the kitchen area and see Randy working. It's about ten o'clock and the breakfast rush has gone by now and Randy is making a big kettle of vegetable soup for the lunch crowd. He asked me last night, after the Sisterhood meeting, if I would be here this morning and I said I would be.

Lizabett and I are both taking a class at Pasadena City College so we meet here afterwards every Monday, Wednesday and Friday morning about this time. Usually Marilee comes out of the diner's office and talks with us. We're a little early today, but she'll be out soon. Sometimes Becca has time off from her internship and can join us, too.

Now and then we head out for lunch at one of the restaurants along Colorado Boulevard—Mi Piace with its white tablecloths or Johnny Rockets with its fifties décor—but usually we're content to just eat at The Pews. It's home to us.

"I read that Lucille Ball once said that she couldn't sing or act either—she couldn't even dance," Lizabett says as she holds up a copy of *Variety* and points to the list of casting calls. "It's all about having the courage to try."

All of us in the Sisterhood have the highest respect for courage. Still... "I don't think things are the same as they were when Lucy first started. Nobody gets anywhere in Hollywood without some talent."

Truth be told, I'm kind of touched by Lizabett's enthusiasm for my acting career. But I've read enough about getting into the movies to be a realist. People have to join SAG—that's the Screen Actor's Guild—to get any good parts. They can hang out and be an extra in movies, but basically all they get is the all-you-can-eat buffet truck and fifty to a hundred dollars for the day. Not many people actually work up to a speaking part that way, which is what a person needs to really be in the movies. Even one spoken word does the trick. Some lucky people go from being an extra to having a bit part and, with a bit part, they have a chance.

I have to admit I've read enough about becoming an actress that I know how it's done.

"You might have talent," Lizabett says stubbornly. "You never know until you try. You could at least audition."

I'm watching the reflection in the other side of the counter so I see Randy walk to the door of the kitchen. "Audition for what?"

Lizabett turns and sees him. "Don't you think Carly would make a great actress?"

"Sure," he says.

Okay, so he's looking at me now in a very nice way. Sort of like he's happy to be my cheerleader.

"Most of the people who audition for things have experience," I say just so no one gets their hopes up.

"So, get some experience," Randy says as he walks over to the counter and leans on the other side of it. You know, I have to say right here that Marilee was right all of those times she went on and on about the grill guy's eyes. He does have these amazing eyes that are blue and gray all swirled together and they crinkle when he smiles. Marilee never said anything about the crinkling. And his hair isn't bad either. It's full and dark and touchable. Not to mention that he's tall, but not too tall. And he moves like an athlete. I don't know that he has a San Marino look, but whatever his look is, it's good.

Okay, so I need to get a grip on myself. I turn to Lizabett. "Things have changed since *I Love Lucy.*"

There's nothing like Lucille Ball to throw some cold water on a fantasy. She might have claimed to make it without talent, but that doesn't really happen.

"Don't worry about that," Lizabett says as she puts the *Variety* down on the counter. "Lucille Ball only *said* she didn't have any talent—everyone knows she really did. We're always our own worst critic. Maybe you have more talent than you think, too. Besides, you just seem like a movie star."

"You're the one who dances, I don't. And I can't sing. I can knit now, but that's only thanks to Rose and I don't think there's a demand to see actresses knit. I don't know what I can do that might be a talent."

"You can walk," Lizabett says firmly.

Both Randy and I look at her.

"Of course I can *walk*."

"No, I mean like a movie star. If you just walk across the screen, people will know you were born to be a star."

"There haven't been silent movies for almost eighty years," I say gently. I hate to be the one to disappoint anyone. "If someone is going to be an actress these days, they need to talk, too. I have a pretty average voice."

Lizabett is hunched over her newspaper scanning the casting calls like she's expecting a miracle.

I hear footsteps in the back of the diner.

"What's up?" Marilee says as she walks toward us. She takes her baseball cap off and shakes her head to make her hair fluff out a little. Marilee used to wear baseball caps all the time and now she only wears them when she's back in her office doing the books for the diner. She says they help her think.

"We're trying to get Carly a place in the movies," Randy says.

I watch Randy looking at Marilee, but the pupils in his eyes don't get bigger or anything. I read once that you can tell if a man is attracted to a woman because his pupils dilate when he looks at her.

"I probably need to have experience before I can get a part," I say, trying to keep a good grasp on reality.

Randy shifts his shoulders so he can look at me while I'm talking. I'm not sure, but I think his pupils do get a little darker. Maybe it's the change in the light, though.

"Here's one you don't need experience to get," Lizabett says as she holds up the newspaper. "It says right here. 'No singing needed.'"

I stop looking at Randy's eyes and look at the newspaper. "But they'd still expect some acting."

Lizabett shakes her head. "It says you need to be calm and able to walk serenely across the stage with a pack attached."

"Well, you can walk serenely, that's for sure," Marilee says. "You had to do that when you were the queen in the Rose Parade. You could even wave at people if you needed to. You did that, too."

"And a pack—that's nothing," Randy adds. "You had to stand for hours on that float with a crown on your head."

"And you like animals," Lizabett says as though that settled everything.

"I have a *cat.* That doesn't mean animals. What kind of a job is that, anyway? I'm not doing a circus show. I'm afraid of heights."

"It's not a circus show," Lizabett says. "It's the Christmas pageant that's going to be at the North Hollywood Cathedral. They're running it just like community theatre with an open casting call and everything."

"Oh, you should try out," Marilee says. "Maybe you could be an angel or something."

I see the crinkles start in Randy's eyes, but he doesn't say anything.

"I'm not sure there's angels," Lizabett says as she frowns at what she's reading in the paper.

"How can it be a Christmas pageant without angels?" Randy looks away from me to ask.

"It says it's a Christmas pageant set in the Dust Bowl of the 1930s—sort of in *The Grapes of Wrath* style with migrant farmworkers. It's written by a novice playwright."

"Really?" For the first time since Lizabett started talking, I'm optimistic. I might be able to do dust in a beginner's play.

"If you want me to go with you to the audition, I will," Marilee volunteers. "I can drive you."

"It's today at three o'clock," Lizabett adds as she hands me the paper. "I'd go, but I have a class."

"Okay," I say and I'm kind of getting excited myself.

If nothing else I will get Sisterhood points for trying something new. Speaking of which, maybe I'll take the journal with me. If I have to sit in a room with the others who are auditioning, I'd like to have something to do. I know that each actress will have to wait her turn to perform before the casting director.

* * *

Hi, this is Marilee. Carly left the journal with me while she went over to stand in the line with the other actresses, so I am sitting here and writing a bit. We made it down to the auditions in Studio City in plenty of time and were even lucky enough to find a parking space on the street. I had never noticed before that Carly does walk like royalty. It must be all the training she had when she was competing for the Rose Queen crown. I wouldn't have known, if she hadn't told me, all that is involved in preparing for that competition. She could have been practicing for the Olympics and not have spent any more effort on it.

Anyway, I'm glad Carly wanted me to come with her. This place is just what I would imagine they would use for something like this. It is a big metal warehouse building with those low-hanging bulbs that give off cold, blue light. It is chilly enough outside that everyone is wearing jackets or sweaters inside, but the light doesn't make it seem any warmer than it is. Maybe they want it to be uncomfortable to weed out the people who aren't serious about auditioning. I look around me. Lots of these people are dressed up like *The Grapes of Wrath* kind of people. I feel an urge to go around and hand out quarters. Or was it dimes, back then?

I've heard some of the people talking and, apparently, the playwright has money to pay actors even though he's never had a play performed before. His uncle's footing the bill. The play might not be prestigious, but it looks like a lot of people want a chance to act in it.

I look at Carly in her designer blue jeans. She doesn't look like anything from that era. Oh, well, it's too late for her to change. Besides, someone had to have nice clothes, even in the Depression.

They have Christmas music playing from speakers here and there. The assistants who are organizing everything are walking around with clipboards and telling people which line to stand in. I lose track of Carly for a minute while she changes lines. She was going to try to get in the angel line, but it looks like the clipboard people told her to get into some other line.

Oh, there she is again. Changing lines must have worked because Carly is walking across the stage right now. She's stopped and is standing in front of the casting director and a few other people. I am too far away to hear what they are saying to her, but I know they're talking because she's nodding her head. A nod should be a positive thing, shouldn't it?

I didn't think I would be this nervous when I came with Carly. Maybe it's just the combined anxiety of all of the others in this warehouse. So many people have dreams in the world and it doesn't seem like there's enough happy endings to go around. I'm not sure that's exactly Biblical. I'll have to ask Pastor Engstrom the next time I meet with his group. It's sort of one of those how-big-is-the-goodness-of-God questions. I know God says He gives us the desires of our hearts, but is a role in a nativity pageant included? I hope so because I have the feeling Carly needs something extra in her life right now. She's worried about something, but she doesn't say anything about it when we ask her.

I know she's been focused on how people see her, but I think the problem may be how she sees herself. I've noticed more and more how the steps we're taking in the Sisterhood are steps we all should have taken a few years ago. We never had the luxury of the usual teenage angst and now it's all piling up on top of us. That's one reason why I wanted us to do this journal. We need a place to grow and, sometimes, a person grows faster when they have a place to think. I know I do and writing in the journal does that for me.

Oh, here comes Carly now. I am going to put the journal away so she knows she has my full attention. Or, better yet, maybe she'll want to write a few words in here since I see she is holding a manila folder in her right hand and the others don't have one. That has to be a good sign, doesn't it?

Hi, this is Carly. Don't get excited. I told Marilee I didn't even want to write it out, but she insisted. So here it is. I got a part, but it's such a small part it shouldn't even be on the list. I am the understudy for Mary. The casting director told me I have the wrong look, the wrong hair, the wrong walk, the wrong everything except for the right height and body type.

I'm going to be the understudy which means I get to watch the play for almost two weeks of rehearsal and three days of live performance and, of course, I get to help the director block out Mary's moves so that the real Mary doesn't have to strain herself by standing in one place too long. If she could ride a donkey when she was nine months pregnant, I would think she could do her own standing.

Well, I suppose the original Mary would have been able to do it. But then again, I don't have a clue what the real Mary was like. Maybe I should find out since I'm going to be standing in for someone pretending to be her. I don't see how Hollywood can do her justice, though, not even if the performance is going to be in a church.

At first, when they said I had the understudy part, I thought I might be on the stage some of the time. But since the play only lasts for a few days, the casting director told me they don't expect the understudies to perform at all. It seems like if I have to do all his work, I should get some credit.

"Let's get out of here," I say as I give Marilee back the pen and the journal.

"You're taking the part, aren't you?" Marilee looks at me with her worried face.

Until Marilee asked, I was thinking of calling the number in the packet when I got home and turning down the offer. Which is probably why Marilee has that look on her face. She knows me too well.

I shake my head. "Yes, of course I am."

When I really think about it, I wouldn't want to disappoint Lizabett or Marilee. "I might learn more about how this is all done and have a better shot at a real part next time."

If I'd known what I was doing, I would have come to the audition looking the part. I would have dyed my hair brown and brought a brown shirt to wear. I guess it must be the dust image, but everywhere I look in this warehouse, I see brown shirts.

"At least they're doing the play in English," I say as Marilee stands. I realize I don't even know what language Mary spoke. I follow Marilee toward the exit door. "And I get a few free tickets so I can give them away to people to come see where the action is that I helped block out in rehearsal. Want to come?"

"Sure," Marilee says as we step outside. "I wouldn't miss it. You're my favorite blocker."

We're already on the 101 Freeway headed back to Pasadena when it occurs to me that I need to decide whether or not to tell my mother what I'm doing. If I do, she'll want to invite the whole town of San Marino to the performance.

My mother has been—how shall I say it—overly anxious to promote me since I was interviewed in the *Pasadena Star News* when my cat ran away. It's a long story, but the important piece is that the reporter took a picture of me in front of my uncle's house and said it was my parent's house. It's a natural mistake because my parents and I have lived with my uncle and aunt for the past twelve years. The house is huge and we have our own set of rooms, but still my aunt was upset that the neighbors might think she and my uncle are the freeloaders when it's me and my parents who are the charity cases.

I told my aunt and mother both that I would call the *Pasadena Star News* and ask them to print a correction, but they were both horrified at that idea. In the meantime, my aunt and my mother are defensive about who is the important one in the house and my mother wants to show that she has something my childless aunt doesn't. Which means she wants to show me off.

My mother and I have been through all of this since the competition for the Rose Queen the fall before I was diagnosed with Hodgkin's disease. I couldn't help but notice that she told all of the neighbors about me being Rose Queen, but refused to tell any of them that I had cancer. Of course, everyone could see I was sick so she told them I had gotten mono from kissing some guy. In her mind, kissing makes everything more glamorous, even diseases.

I didn't know about the mono story until I started getting these fluffy little "get well" cards and my mother told me what she'd done. I tried to tell her there was no shame in having cancer, but I could tell she didn't really believe me. In her mind, there was shame in being imperfect and I had to admit she was right there. I could no longer even pretend to be her perfect little daughter.

I used to think my mother would become used to imperfection because of my dad's drinking problem, but she hasn't. As far as I know, she hasn't told anyone, except for me and my aunt and uncle, that my dad has been in and out of an alcohol rehab center this past year. Somehow she must think that, if she doesn't say something aloud, it won't be true. I'm not even sure she's completely accepted that my dad is an alcoholic and needs help.

Sometimes I wonder if I'm waiting to become perfect before I move out of my uncle's house. I got my cat because I wanted to move out and get a place of my own. But my mother looked so horrified when I mentioned I might leave that I decided to wait a while longer, especially because my dad has been gone for a couple of months in this latest rehab phase of his. That must mean he's getting better this time. When he comes back, maybe that will be a good time for me to move. I would hate to leave my mother alone.

Chapter Three

> "In spite of everything, I still believe that people are really good at heart. I simply can't build my hopes on a foundation consisting of confusion, misery and death."
>
> —*Anne Frank*

One day Marilee brought us this quote. She had printed it out by hand in big block letters and said she was going to put it over her desk in the diner to remind herself that everyone needs hope. The one thing we all learned from cancer was that we could only be distressed for so long. Then we had to reign in our terror and find hope somewhere. We talked about Anne Frank that night. For the first time, we felt like we were the fortunate ones. At least this thing trying to kill us was a disease and not the people we used to sit next to in school.

* * *

I don't know that it's a good thing this was the quote that came into my mind when I sat down to write about my new acting job. Marilee and I got back to the diner in time for us to have a salad before I needed to go home. The more time that has passed since I auditioned for the part of Mary in the play, the more I am glad that I got the understudy part instead of the real thing.

I'm torn. If I had the regular part, I might disappoint people. And there's my secrets. I'm not sure I want to pretend to be something I'm not anymore. Besides, the audience might expect Mary to have a glow about her and I wouldn't blame them. She had to have something special. She talked to an angel. That would make a girl stand up tall. It's much safer to be on the sidelines watching someone else portraying the woman who gave birth to the baby who changed the world than it is to be front and center oneself.

That's heavy-duty stuff.

I didn't realize quite what I might have gotten into until I talked to Randy. He asked me if I had a ride home and Marilee said she would like to do some grocery shopping so, if Randy could drop me off, that would be helpful.

I know Marilee only said that so Randy would take me home. Oh, she'll stop at a grocery store on her way home. Marilee wouldn't lie. She's just not above arranging her schedule so that Randy and I spend some time together.

Randy has a stripped-down white Jeep. He parked it behind the diner in the spot that belongs to Uncle Lou.

"Let me get that," Randy says as he walks around to open the door to the Jeep.

The night is dark and cold. It feels a little damp like it might rain later. Colorado Boulevard is quiet tonight. There is a streetlamp giving off a dim light.

Randy has to move some snorkeling gear into the backseat so I can sit in the passenger seat.

"Sorry about that," he mumbles.

"It's okay," I say and, to tell the truth, I am kind of relieved to see the gear sitting in the passenger seat. That means this is just a casual offer to help a friend; it's not something he had planned in advance. I never liked dating campaigns; they always make me nervous.

I have the Sisterhood journal with me and I lay it flat on my lap.

"I didn't know you snorkel," I say after he walks around to the driver's door and gets in the Jeep.

"You'll have to come with me sometime," Randy says as he turns the ignition key and looks behind him so he can back up and turn around. "Even if you don't snorkel, the beach is good."

"Sounds nice," I say and then wait a minute. "I'll probably have to dye my hair brown for the play."

"Makes sense," Randy says as he turns onto Colorado Boulevard.

I smile to myself. He passed the blond test. I don't

know why guys always think blond and beach in the same sentence, but when he invited me snorkeling I wondered if he had some particular picture in his mind. But Randy doesn't sound like he cares what color of hair I have. Which is good. Maybe he's not like some of the other guys I've dated.

"I might need to get some freckles, too," I say.

"Mary had freckles?" Randy looks over at me in surprise.

I shrug. "Maybe." She would if she had been me.

I don't know anything about what Mary looked like or how she felt. I can't help but wonder, though, if she felt as cozy riding beside Joseph on that donkey of hers that starry night long ago as I feel tonight riding beside Randy in this Jeep. I'm thinking, after my conversation with Marilee last night, that maybe I should get to know Randy a little better. Marilee has found her guy in Quinn. I need to accept that. Maybe I need to stop running and give Randy a chance.

I grab the journal a little tighter as it sits in my lap. I'm going to need to write some more before tomorrow. Surprisingly, the pages are filling up even though last night, I didn't write at all because my mother was upset when I got home. My aunt had left a note telling us that the house was going to be part of the San Marino Holiday Home and Garden tour this year, just like it has been in past years, so we would need to use the side entrance to the house next Saturday.

My parents and I always use the side entrance so my mother says my aunt just left that note to remind us of our place.

When I get a good job, I'm going to buy a house so my parents will have their own place and can use the front door. It might not be in San Marino though. Not many people can afford to buy houses here.

I have to tell you about my uncle's place. It's a three-story house with forty-five hundred square feet on each level. An army could live in it. The main floor has a master bedroom suite in addition to three living rooms, a dining room large enough to fit a twenty-foot table, and a kitchen. The maid has a bedroom and bath for her use behind the pantry. The housekeeper lives out.

The second floor is mostly suites of bedrooms—there are seven suites total, each with a bedroom, bathroom and second room. The suites used by my parents and me are at the opposite end of the house from the rooms used when my aunt and uncle have company. We seldom take our meals with my uncle and aunt anyway, but we definitely do not when they have guests. We double definitely do not if my father has been drinking, which seems to be all the time when he's home.

I wonder if my aunt and uncle will have visitors for Christmas this year. Sometimes they do. I like it when they do because my aunt scents the air with this special cinnamon and the fumes come up to my rooms. One year I learned the word *redolent* just to describe it. I can still remember going to sleep with that smell in the air.

My uncle's house is always decorated for Christmas. The housekeeper puts white twinkling lights around all of the windows and hangs big pine wreaths in all of the windows in the downstairs. All of the decorations are the best money can buy; my aunt sees to that because of the tour. There's enough gold foil and bright lights tucked around the house to make it all look like the Christmas window in Tiffany's in New York. The whole thing glitters.

"Some place," Randy says as he turns into the driveway of my uncle's house. The drive goes in a half circle so that cars can drop off someone and not have to back up or turn around or anything as lower class as that.

Randy stops by the front porch and turns off the Jeep's ignition.

This is always the awkward part of having a guy bring me home. It's not that I'm worried about whether or not the guy will kiss me. It's that I can never think of any graceful way to say that I don't go in the front door of this house. I have keys for a side entrance. It's not that I mind telling people about the doors; it's just that I don't want to then have to answer any questions about how the arrangement came to be.

This isn't the first time Randy has been to my uncle's house. He and the whole Sisterhood were out here looking in all of the trees when my cat ran away. Even when Marie was missing, though,

Randy didn't look at my uncle's house and frown like he's doing now.

Randy looks over at me and swallows. "I grew up in Fontana. In a trailer park." He pauses and looks up at the house again. "I just thought you should know."

I smile. Sometimes I'm brave. "It's my uncle's house."

Just like that, I said it. My mother would be appalled that I told anyone.

I decide to add to it, "If it wasn't for my uncle, I would be homeless. My parents, too. There's nothing wrong with a trailer park."

"Really?"

I nod. "Really. At least you had your own place and didn't have to worry about being told to leave."

I can see Randy is relieved, and that makes me feel good. If he doesn't care whether I'm blond or rich, he's definitely not like the other guys I've dated.

This is the first time a guy walks me to the door and it is the right door. We talk for a while, just standing on the steps, and I explain more about how it is with my uncle. Then we talk about me playing the Mary role and how people might expect me to be perfect if I had that part. Since I've spent so much time trying to be perfect, I wonder if it's a good role for me. Talking to Randy feels good. The fact that he kisses me doesn't hurt either.

Randy is long gone and I'm getting ready for bed before I remember that I have the journal and meant to write in it tonight. It'll have to wait for tomorrow.

* * *

Hi, this is Carly again. I came down to The Pews this morning after my Saturday class. Becca and Marilee are going to meet me here for lunch, but I am early so I'm writing in the journal.

I'm starting an English literature major at Pasadena City College, incidentally. I'm five years behind my original schedule because of what we in the Sisterhood call IDC, or interruption due to cancer, but I'm getting it done.

I'm not as career-focused as Becca is. She went after the internship of hers with everything she had. She really wants to be a lawyer or a judge. It might sound corny, but Becca is determined to make the world right, and I applaud her. She'll learn a lot working as an intern with that judge.

I don't know what I will do with my degree, but I thought that I couldn't go wrong learning more about books. I love books. After the past few days, I've wondered if I was drawn to English literature because of all of the drama that surrounds me.

I thought about secrets last night. When I think about it rationally, I realize it is silly for my mother to want us all to keep it a secret that we are living in my uncle's house and have no actual home of our own. I don't even know why I have gone along with it for the past twelve years. When we moved into my uncle's house, I was in junior high school. Back then, I thought my mother kept our housing arrangement a secret because she worried I might feel bad if my school friends knew we didn't have our own house.

Since I went to school in San Marino, all of my classmates had families with huge houses. I'll admit I might have felt a little strange back then if people knew I had nothing, especially because my father was having a hard time finding jobs then and his drinking problem was starting to become much worse.

I don't need to impress anyone now, though. I have known that the Sisterhood wouldn't care if my parents own a house or if my father makes a dime. I really can't think of one good reason that I've kept it a secret all of these years.

Except for my mother. Sometimes I wonder if my mother is well.

I have such ambivalent feelings toward my mother that I don't even like to talk about it with anyone. Once in a while, I make a comment in the Sisterhood meetings and the others ask a question or two inviting me to speak more about it, but I can't quite wrap any words around it. It's hard when your mother lives for you. It feels very ungrateful to complain. It's not like she's ignoring you. It's the opposite, in fact.

I wonder how Mary in the Bible got along with her mother. Did she tell her mother about the visit from the angel?

My mother would be all over it if I'd had a visit like that. She'd want to impress the neighbors. Of course, my mother wouldn't like the being-pregnant part. So she'd be torn since she couldn't really tell everyone about the angel visit without mentioning what the angel said. People would definitely want to know that.

Oh, I see Becca now. She's just opened the door and is in the outer part of the diner. She's heading back this way.

"Law!" Becca exclaims as she opens the French doors to the place where the Sisterhood meets. She uses a tone of voice usually reserved for members of the opposite sex by both sexes when they're annoyed. She's got her dark hair tucked back to show off her long silver earrings.

I'm used to Becca talking about the law, but usually she seems in favor of it, especially now that she has this internship. "Something wrong?"

Becca shakes her head as she sits down in one of the chairs around the table. "I can't believe the judge did that."

Having said that, Becca stands up again, looking like a warrior, and begins to pace. "It's not right to let that man go free."

I'm assuming something happened in the internship Becca has.

The room is not wide enough for Becca to pace for long so I stand up and move a chair that's in her way. "What happened?"

"Some policeman forgot to read the man his rights when he arrested him."

"I'm sure that happens."

Becca stops pacing and looks at me. If I'm not mistaken there's a tear in one of her eyes. "The law is supposed to give everyone justice. That poor girl he beat up isn't getting justice. Not with him walking away on some technicality."

"Oh, that's bad."

Becca nods. I see the tear start to fall. I wish Marilee were here. She's so much better at comforting than I am. I see another tear fall on the other cheek. What can I do? I open my arms.

It's hard to see the polish come off of a dream. Even something like the law isn't always perfect.

Becca and I sit together for a while. We both have our knitting with us and eventually we take it out and start to knit. We've knitted out our problems so many times it's almost second nature to us.

"They'll catch him on something else," Becca finally says. She's doing a purl-stitch pattern so she needs to concentrate. "I just hope that no one gets hurt next time. He can't just go around beating up on people who are standing in a doorway he thinks belongs to him."

"At least he got a good scare," I add. "If he has any sense, he'll think twice before he attacks anyone again."

"And the judge does have to uphold the law." Becca finishes a row.

"It's for the greater good," I say.

Becca nods and then looks up at me. "But that poor girl."

I nod.

Becca continues, "She reminded me of Lizabett when she was so sick. Remember when we first knew her, how pale she looked? And, on top of that, I think this girl is homeless."

"Surely, if the girl is sick someone's taking care of her."

"She was in county hospital for a bit, but I don't think she has anyone. She told them she was eighteen, but she doesn't look more than sixteen. She wasn't even supposed to be there in the courthouse, but she came in when the judge was dismissing the charges and said it wasn't fair. They made her leave, but I got to talk to her in the hallway."

"The poor thing."

"I told her that if she came by The Pews to eat, she could mention my name and I'd pay for her bill. I told Randy about it so he's going to look for her."

"That's good."

"She said the hospital shaved her head to put on a bandage."

"Oh, dear."

"But she didn't have a bandage that I could see. I suppose she could have had a bad case of head lice, but I don't think so."

"Oh."

Becca looks at me and I look at her. We are thinking the same thing. We know about baldness.

"I don't think she's on chemo," Becca finally

says. "The hospital wouldn't let a person with cancer live on the streets, would they?"

"I don't know."

It's not often I see Becca look defeated.

"Maybe she'll come in here and we can find out more about her," I say. I look out the glass in the French doors hoping for a glimpse of Marilee. Marilee and Lizabett should both be here by now.

I reach over and pat Becca on the shoulder. "Maybe she's just got a flu bug or something. That can make a person's face look drained and pale. And the bald head could be a fashion statement."

"Her name's Joy," Becca says. "She told me that like it's a joke."

I look up at the French doors again. "Ah, here comes Marilee."

I knew Marilee would know how to comfort Becca. Even though she had this yank-the-sliver-out philosophy, Becca had been just as scared as the rest of us when we had our cancers. Becca and I were the ones who didn't like to show our emotions, though, especially not when we thought we might die. Marilee was the one who taught us both how to cry when we needed the tears.

No one can see it, but I'm crying now. All for a girl named Joy. I haven't met her, but I feel like I know her. Both Becca and I know how cancer changes a person's face. It is in the skin color and the eyes and, if there's any left, in the hair.

I hope Joy does come into The Pews. As awful

as it is to have cancer, it must be one hundred times worse to have cancer when you're homeless.

Marilee has her arm around Becca now and I can see Becca relax.

I pick up my knitting, but I don't have any heart for pushing a needle into yarn. I look through the glass in the French doors and see that people are starting to come in for lunch. I know they are short a waitress out front, so I decide to go out and help.

All of us in the Sisterhood know our way around The Pews and have filled in when Uncle Lou has needed extra help. The one waitress out front will probably be able to handle the customers, but I'd like to be busy for a while. Whenever I think about dying of cancer, I like to get up and move my body just to remind myself that I can.

I tell Marilee and Becca what I'm doing and stand up to walk through the doors.

I hope Joy comes in. That will make Becca feel better.

When I'm on the other side of the French doors, I turn around and see Marilee and Becca with their heads bowed. They must be praying for Joy. It's the first time I've been on this side of the French doors, looking back, and I feel left out. We never used to pray in the Sisterhood, at least not together. It had never occurred to me when Marilee said she was a Christian that it might be something that could come between us in the Sisterhood. Are we going to have those who pray and those who can only look on in bewilderment? It might not just be my secrets that could pull us apart.

I'm still thinking about that when I wrap a dish towel around my waist and get ready to take orders. Uncle Lou has these giant white dish towels that everyone uses for aprons. They're cotton so they wash up nice.

I wonder if Marilee will want to pray about my problems some day. If she asks me, I don't know if I'll say go ahead or not. I don't think I've ever been prayed over before. I'm not sure how it would feel.

Chapter Four

"To sit in the shade on a fine day and look upon verdure is the most perfect refreshment."
—Jane Austen

We were starting to recover from our chemo treatments when Lizabett brought this quote to the Sisterhood meeting. It reminded us of an exercise Rose had us do where we closed our eyes and pictured our perfect scene. We were all supposed to know our perfect scene well enough that we could put it into our minds when we felt sick.

Lizabett said her scene was a Jane Austen moment that she'd seen at Huntington Botanical Gardens one day. She had to explain to us that verdure meant lush green landscape and that she'd seen some ladies sitting on the lawn by the duck pond in old-fashioned hats. Someone was painting them and it all looked very English garden. That was Lizabett's scene.

Becca pictured the ocean down at Crystal Cove; she used to go there and walk along the beach for hours. I've been there, too. Old cottages line that beach and remind you of the families who lived there years ago.

For her scene, Marilee saw her mother sitting beside the fireplace in their house in Pasadena. She said her mother was always reading a book and everything felt safe.

I, Carly, saw the night sky, looking straight up in the cloudless dark with the stars sprinkled around.

Tonight, I see my night sky. It's not always easy to see the stars in Pasadena, but sometimes in San Marino you can because there are fewer streetlights here. There's a small balcony at the end of the hallway on the second floor of my uncle's house and sometimes, if I can't sleep, I will go sit on a chair on that balcony and look up at the sky. Tonight I brought the journal with me. It's too dark to read anything, but I left the hall light on and I wrote anyway.

I just had to get down what happened. I only spent a few minutes waiting tables in The Pews before Becca and Marilee came out of the Sisterhood room and were ready to go to lunch. I wouldn't think much could happen in a few minutes, but it did. I'd felt a little shy when I went into the kitchen because Randy was there and we'd kissed last night when he drove me home. Some people think I've kissed lots of guys, but I haven't. Besides, Randy feels special to me and I was wondering if he'd give some sign that I was special to him.

I was thinking maybe he'd wink at me or give me a long, smoldering look. Or even come right out and just say that last night was very nice. But he didn't do any of those things.

I sure wasn't expecting what he did instead.

Randy asked me if I wanted to live in an apartment he has on top of his diner in West Hollywood.

"But I have a place," I said without even thinking about it.

"I thought you might like to have your *own* place," Randy said. He had a white chef's cap on and he was grilling some of Uncle Lou's famous hamburgers. He flipped a couple of buns and then looked at me. "You wouldn't need to worry about rent. I wouldn't charge anything. The place has been empty for a while. Of course, you'd have to like to watch sporting events on television."

"Really, my uncle's house isn't bad."

Randy flipped a hamburger. "Well, think about it. It's there if you change your mind."

I couldn't wait to get my dish towel unwrapped from my waist so I could go out the door with Becca and Marilee. The day was gray and we started walking up Colorado Boulevard toward the Paseo mall. We like the Thai place that's a couple of blocks away and that's where we'd talked about going for Pad Thai noodles and lemongrass soup.

"Feeling better?" I ask Becca. She's looking

better, but I don't want to just jump into my problems. We're big on little courtesies like that in the Sisterhood.

Becca nods. "I just hope Joy goes by The Pews."

We're walking single file down the sidewalk so I can't see Becca's face.

"I bet she will," I say.

We walk past a candle store and the air smells of a dozen kinds of musky scents.

"Guess what?" I say after a minute.

Both Marilee and Becca turn to look at me.

I am trying my best to let the Sisterhood see deeper into my life. "Randy offered me an apartment to stay in. Over his diner in West Hollywood."

"With him?" Becca says and I have her full attention now. She's stopped walking and is frowning. "I don't know that—"

"I don't think it's with him," I say. "He said it was empty and that, if I liked to watch sports on television, it could be mine."

Marilee is standing still, too. "Well, if he cares about what you watch on television, he must live there, too. Why else would he ask about that? Maybe he means he has an empty *room* you could have."

Marilee is shaking her head, but she doesn't look jealous.

"Of course, it would be your decision," Becca says a little stiffly.

"I told him no, anyway. He was only offering it so I could have a place of my own."

"Why would you move?" Marilee says. "You've got that big house with your parents in San Marino. Who would leave that? You've got trees and everything."

Here is the moment I've been waiting for. The moment when I tell the Sisterhood that I'm not the rich person they think I am. Which shouldn't be so hard because I know they don't care if I have a dollar to my name. It's just that I haven't told them for so long that I wonder what they will think of me for not telling them sooner.

Just then a woman comes up to us with bags swinging from both of her arms and we need to move so she can pass. After we move, we all start walking again and the moment to tell them about the house is gone. We have to sit at a long table in the Thai place so we aren't even facing each other. It doesn't feel like the time to announce I have been an imposter for years.

I wonder if I could tell everyone in an e-mail. I could say: "Hello, this is Carly. I know you don't care where I live, but—" No, that isn't right. I don't want to imply that the Sisterhood doesn't care. Even Randy cares. At least, I hope so, otherwise his offer of an apartment or room or whatever is not such a good one. I know most guys would make that kind of an offer because they expected you to live with them in the apartment. As in *live with them.* I don't think that's what Randy was thinking, though. Of course, it's what the Sisterhood is thinking now and, unless I tell them what I told Randy about how it feels to live in my uncle's house, they'll continue to think that.

I really think Randy is just being kind.

I'll definitely have to tell the Sisterhood about my uncle's house. But after we split the check, Becca needs to go to a dental appointment and Marilee wants to stop and visit her dad at the auto dealership on Colorado. Now that she and her dad are getting along better, Marilee doesn't need anyone with her for that visit. So I go back to The Pews and wait tables for a little longer before I go back home. All the time, I'm thinking about how I can word my confession to the Sisterhood.

That's not the only reason I'm sitting out here on the balcony trying to find the stars in the night sky, though. It's my mother. She found a flyer from the play I'm going to be working on. It's called *The Dust Bowl Nativity* and I could see my mother frowning as she read about it. The flyer was printed on brown recycled paper with black ink. My mother likes her advertisements in full color on high-gloss paper.

"I was going to tell you," I say to her. I'd set my books down on the table in the room my parents and I share as a living room. We have a burgundy leather sofa and chair set that was passed down to us after my aunt's latest remodeling project downstairs. "It's a play. I'm going to be Mary's understudy."

I had stopped at the refrigerator outside this room on my way in and I had a pear in my hand. It was an imported pear, of course. My mother will not buy any common fruit because she heard once that we are what we eat and she doesn't want us to eat fruit that isn't good enough for us.

"Mary, like in the Bible?" My mother's frown clears. She sits down on the sofa, still holding the flyer in her hand.

I nod. "It's only an understudy part, but I have tickets if you want to see the play. Maybe Dad will be home by then and he can go, too."

I take a bite out of the pear and, once I break the skin, the air smells of the fruit.

"Of course I want to see the play. I always said you'd do well in Hollywood. Your aunt should see this, too. It's not every day a Winston stars in a play."

Part of me isn't surprised she doesn't mention my father. I can't let her continue to think this play is bigger than it is though. "It's a small production. Experimental theatre. And I won't be starring."

"Don't let them kid you. If it's any kind of a nativity play, Mary is the primary person. Without her, what do they have? Some man walking across a desert beside a donkey."

"I'm the understudy. That means I only go onstage if the regular actress is sick or something." I see my mother's face. "Which won't happen. The play isn't going to be around long enough for someone to catch the flu or anything. The director already told me not to count on any stage time."

"They didn't choose you to be the lead?" My mother looks up at me as though she just now understands. "Who do they think they are?"

"You know how it is, Mom."

I take another bite of pear.

"Are they blind?"

"It's not easy to get a part in a play."

"Did you tell them you were the Rose Parade Queen? You're not just a beginner, you know." My mother is frowning at me again. "Those are called fragrant pears. They're grown to be particularly juicy."

I take a tissue from the box on the table beside the sofa and hold it in my hand to catch some of the juice.

"Maybe next time I'll have a better part," I say as I take a final bite of the pear.

"I just wish—" my mother begins and then stops.

My mother doesn't finish her sentence, but she doesn't really need to. I know her wishes. She wishes that everything were perfect. Me. The role. The play. The way things were perfect before our problems started. The house, the cancer, my dad's drinking.

None of it's perfect anymore, especially me. Not that I was perfect before I had cancer, but my mother thought I was close enough that it kept her world balanced. When I was declared cancer-free, I thought my mother would mentally put me back on the pedestal she had me on before. I didn't exactly want back on the pedestal, but some days now I think it would be easier than dealing with my mother's continual disappointment in me.

My fall from grace was not gradual. It came the day I became sick.

I wrap the core of the pear in the tissue in my hand.

"How was your day?" I say to my mother, hoping to move her mind off of my imperfections and onto the routine imperfections of the rest of her day. "Did you talk to the man at the dry-cleaning place?"

My mother takes her dry cleaning to this place every Friday and picks it up every Saturday.

"He said my blue knit needs some repair."

I nod. My mother has a series of suits that she wore to her last job, which was as a secretary. She hasn't worked since we came to live in my uncle's house. She makes a great show of examining the *Los Angeles Times* classified ads every Sunday afternoon, but none of the jobs meet her requirements. They don't pay enough or sound important enough or have enough advancement possibilities. Still, even though she never applies for any of the jobs, she insists on keeping her suits ready. She rotates the suits for dry cleaning and, of late, the report from the cleaner has been that they need repair.

"The dry cleaners didn't do a good job on the last bit of mending, though, so I don't know. They didn't even match the color right."

For the first time in my life, I notice that my mother is looking old. She's only in her mid-forties, but she has a look about her as she talks about her blue knit suit that makes me think of parchment in a museum. Her face has a frail look like she's ninety. She has made a career out of being grateful to her brother for supporting all of us. He pays for our bills and my father's rehab. I wonder if my mother would look younger if we didn't rely on my uncle quite so much. That thought makes me feel disloyal, though. My mother has done everything she could for us all.

"Maybe I could fix it for you," I say with a nod at the suit.

My mother looks at me as though I offered to fly to the moon and get her a hunk of green cheese for her dinner.

"You know I knit," I remind her.

"Of course," my mother says. "The group you have with those friends of yours."

My mother gives a wave of her hand.

I nod. She never has learned to call us the Sisterhood of the Dropped Stitches. In the past, I've wondered if she has a block in her mind about the Sisterhood because it was part of my cancer days. She never liked anything that had to do with my cancer.

"I'm going to invite my Sisterhood friends to the play, too. I know they'd like to meet you and Dad."

"Your dad won't be back by then."

"Oh." I can't remember the exact date when my dad left to go to the rehab place, but I miss him. "He must be still doing good there."

My dad calls every week or so and talks to my mom. Usually, I'm not home when he calls, but I have managed to talk to him a couple of times and he sounds more sober than he has in years. When I miss the call, my mother tells me what my dad said.

"It would be lovely to see your friends," my mother says, sounding like it would be anything but lovely.

Still, she should meet them. Judging by the look on her face, she might just back out of going. Then she asks me, "Are you going to invite that guy, too?"

"What guy?"

"The one who walked you to the door the other night," my mother says. "I heard his voice when you were talking."

Fortunately, I know my mother could hear the sounds of us talking, but there's no way she could have heard the actual words we said. I'm glad of that.

"I'm not sure Randy can come."

My mother didn't press me on it, but it's all enough to have me sitting up here on the balcony looking for the stars when I should be in bed sleeping. Everything around me feels like it's going to change or has already changed and I just haven't noticed until today. My mother isn't seeing me clearly. Marilee is off talking to God somewhere. Becca, who never falters, is upset about justice.

And Randy either wants to be my knight in shining amour and rescue me or he is expecting something of a physical nature in return for a place to stay and he's the last person I should trust. I wish I knew for sure what his motive is.

Some days I don't know much about anything

when it comes to my life. These are the times when I like to look up at the night sky. I see a few faint stars and something that looks like a bright star, but is moving so fast it has to be an airplane. I can't help but wonder as I look up if God is up there looking down at me as I try to keep my toes warm by curling them into the hem of this old flannel robe.

I'd like to think He sits at the edge of heaven and looks down at someone like me. I give Him the Rose Queen wave just in case He is looking. He doesn't send a thunderbolt down on me for my nerve or anything, so maybe He's not as much like my uncle as I thought. It'd be kind of nice to think He might even be waving back. I wonder if there's a God wave.

I look down at the robe. I have a couple of satin robes in my closet with matching nightgowns. But, when I'm upset, I always reach for this old flannel robe. It used to belong to my dad and my mom gave it to me when I was sick with chemo so I wouldn't ruin my nice robes. This robe and I have been through a lot together.

Now, it comforts me. Maybe things will seem a little more normal tomorrow. Lizabett is supposed to meet me at The Pews for lunch. Maybe I'll ask her to write in the journal so you'll see it's not just me that thinks things are changing. Of course, Lizabett always seems to think things are changing. Maybe it's because she's the youngest and always feels like she's scrambling to keep up with everyone else.

* * *

Hi, this is Lizabett and it is Sunday morning. Carly let me read some of what she's been saying (there are a couple of stapled pages which are a no-read for the Sisterhood so I didn't see those, but I saw the rest). I have to admit that I am a little worried about things changing, too. Not for all of the same reasons as Carly is worried. With me, it's my brother.

I've gotten used to Quinn being a Christian so I'm not so worried about that, but I've never had to sit on the sidelines while Quinn has been in love before and I find that I miss my brother. He used to nag me all the time, but now he doesn't seem to even notice me. I coughed the other day three times and he didn't even seem to hear me. I thought I would like that, but, well, I don't completely. I miss the old mother hen. That's what I call him when he worries about me.

Guys are a mystery, aren't they? Whether they're related or not. I heard about Randy's offer to Carly even before I read about it in the journal. Carly seems to think it's just a generous offer, but I think I'll have Quinn talk to Randy. None of us want Carly going out with some guy who is going to rush her into doing something she'll regret. Besides, they haven't even gone on a real date.

I don't think Carly is considering Randy's offer, but she shouldn't. She's going to be the understudy for Mary. That should mean something, especially on a Sunday morning like today.

Carly and I walked down to that little French bakery and had croissants and jam for breakfast. Then we came back to our room at The Pews to start getting Carly ready for her part in the play. I borrowed some of Quinn's books for our research. I know how it is for actresses. They have to feel their part. Even Lucille Ball had to know what character she was playing. It's even more important for Carly because she's playing Mary, the mother of Jesus, and everyone in the whole world probably has some opinion about what Mary was like. Most of the pictures I've seen of her just show her with her head bowed, but I don't think any mother of a young child spends her life with her head looking down like that even if the baby in her arms were Jesus.

I'm not too sure how it would be for a young mother to hold the baby Jesus.

Fortunately, the play doesn't spend much time on that part, so Carly won't have to be a convincing mother.

Not that she has to be a convincing anything since she's only the understudy.

One thing I know for sure though is that Carly would wow everyone if she just had a chance to walk across the stage. I wonder if the real Mary was as pretty as Carly. Of course there's the glowing-Madonna thing the original Mary had going. It would be hard to compete with that.

When I first met Carly years ago, I envied her. I wanted to have hair like hers. I wanted to have fingernails like hers. And her clothes—I wanted to dress like her.

Carly is definitely the prettiest of us all. And, it's more than that. She just looks expensive.

The surprising thing for me as I got to know Carly, though, was that the best part of Carly is herself. She doesn't know how special she is. Sometimes people get so stuck on looking at her hair and her clothes that they don't take the time to look at her. But they should. Carly is at the top of my list. That's why I think she should be a star.

Chapter Five

"Move Queen Anne? Most certainly not! Why it might some day be suggested that my statue should be moved, which I should much dislike."

—*Queen Victoria when asked about moving a statue of Queen Anne for her own Diamond Jubilee*

One of our rules in the Sisterhood is to treat each other as we would like to be treated. Rose, our counselor, brought this Queen Victoria quote to us one day early on in the Sisterhood meetings. Rose wanted us to know that we are a group of equals and need to treat each other that way. Just like the queens had done. We made ourselves a crown that night out of yellow yarn and passed it from head to head to show we were all the queen. I had more fun with that crown than I did with the one I wore as the Rose Queen.

* * *

I learned that night that it's easy to be queen if you don't mind sharing the crown.

There is nothing equal in the theatre. This is Carly and I'm taking a break to write in the journal while Lizabett makes a couple of phone calls. I never knew Mary was so important. Of course, I knew she gave birth to Jesus, but it didn't end there.

I was half joking earlier about what my mother would tell the neighbors if I had a visit from an angel, but as Lizabett and I have been digging into the books she has, I'm beginning to wonder what Mary's mother could have possibly thought.

I've never thought about Mary's mother before.

I don't even know what I would think if I had a daughter. Lizabett is back and sitting back down at the table again. We don't say anything and Lizabett keeps looking at the books.

One of the books I read earlier tells about Mary. I knew she was young, but I had no idea she was probably thirteen or fourteen. I guess they didn't have Children's Protective Services back then. And I knew she was unmarried, but I had no idea she was engaged to be married.

"Her mother can't have known about the angel visit," I say to Lizabett, putting down the journal. "If she did, she would have forbidden Mary to keep talking to the angel."

Joseph was a good catch. He seemed prosperous and kind. Surely, her mother knew the angel's prophesy could change everything between Joseph and Mary. If Mary's mother was anything like mine, Mary would have been grounded until she forgot all about the angel. Most mothers want their daughters to marry the dependable guy and not listen to the angel.

"And look at all the blue."

I don't know what it is with all of the blue, but as I look at picture after picture of Mary, I see her wearing so many shades of blue. Sky-blue. Robin's egg–blue. Powder-blue. I think the wardrobe person should pay attention to Mary's blue in the play. I wonder if Mary ever really even had a light blue garment. I know they had dye back then, but dyed cloth would be more expensive. Except for Mary's clothes, all the material in the play was brown. Maybe the dust look will be more accurate than blue would have been.

But then maybe Mary came from a rich family. Maybe she had the San Marino address of her day. It doesn't say any place that she had to be poor exactly. Maybe a light blue dyed robe was like having a Gucci handbag for her.

"Imagine having a secret like that?" Lizabett says as she sets down the book she's looking at.

Well, I can certainly imagine having some secrets. "She wouldn't be the first young teenager, not even in a good neighborhood, to be pregnant before she got married."

"Yeah, but to be pregnant because of God! While

you're still a virgin!" Lizabett is looking a little shell-shocked herself. "That'd be like—I don't know what it would be like. People wouldn't even believe her, would they?"

"No more than you'd believe me if I said I was having Elvis Presley's baby."

"But Elvis Presley is dead."

"I know. That's the point. It's impossible."

Lizabett shakes her head. "No wonder Mary didn't tell anyone."

I've been flipping through a book of nativity paintings and reading about the symbolism in the paintings. "I don't even think she told Joseph about the angel's visit."

"Wow."

"She must have been lonely," I say, thinking of the secrets I've kept. Secrets never make you feel closer to anyone. You've always got that hidden thing between you and them.

"I'd rather be lonely though than tell my fiancé that I was pregnant, especially because he'd know he wasn't the father. He probably wouldn't believe the God thing."

"This does sound like great stuff for a play, doesn't it?" I look up from my book. "I never knew it was so filled with drama. It could be *Days of Our Lives.*"

"I can't wait to see the play," Lizabett says. "You're going to be a great Mary."

"Understudy," I correct her. "I'll be the understudy."

Lizabett nods. "But maybe someone will get sick. The flu's going around. I'm not giving up hope."

After reading up on Mary, I must admit I would kind of like to play the part of being her. Not because I expect to have a holy glow or anything. But I would like to get inside Mary's skin like a good actress is supposed to do with a role.

Lizabett and I are still reading away when Marilee and Quinn come. I know they've been to church and I check to see if Marilee has any kind of holy glow about her because she went. She doesn't and it's too bad because I'd like to see some of this glow Mary must have had. Since Marilee and Quinn are here, the four of us move to a table out in the dining part of The Pews.

I don't know why the Sisterhood never eats at our table when we have an outsider with us. We never talk about it; we just make the move out when we have company.

Marilee had called Becca on her way over to The Pews, so Becca is going to join us in a few minutes. The Pews is fairly crowded, but we get a table close to the counter. We gather six chairs, because Randy is going to sit with us as well. It's going to be a regular party.

"I think Randy still has his spicy cheese-and-chilies burger on the specials board," Marilee says. Quinn is the only one who bothers to look at the menu folder at the end of the table. "I think he's got enough of that imported cheese to do the Italian tuna melt, too. That one was my creation."

"I didn't think Uncle Lou let anyone mess with the menu," Lizabett says.

Marilee grins. "That's why it's a good time to try out a few things. Italy's far enough away he can't drop in for lunch. I think we had the whole Pasadena police force in here for that spicy burger. It's something Randy fixes at his diner and it goes over big there."

Randy comes out of the kitchen and heads for our table. He smiles when he sees us. Lizabett nudges me with her elbow. Okay, so maybe she's right and he's smiling at *me* instead of *us*.

The waitress, Linda, comes over to get our order.

"How's the rehearsing going?" Randy asks as he pulls out the chair next to me.

"We're trying to develop the character," Lizabett says. "You know, to get inside Mary's head."

"She was amazing," I add as Randy slides his chair in beside me.

It strikes me at that very moment that Mary never got to go on a date in her life. I know they didn't do that sort of thing back then anyway, but I have to say she missed out on some of the best times. When Randy slid his chair in, he slid it a little closer to me. We're pretty crowded at the table anyway, so it doesn't seem too obvious when he puts his arm around the back of my chair. At least, I don't think it's too obvious.

No one is looking at us anyway. I guess Marilee and Lizabett decided to look at the menu after all.

The next thing I know the door to the diner opens and Becca storms inside.

"Guess who I found?" Becca demands as she walks to the table.

With Becca, it could be anyone, but I take one look at the girl who comes in the door behind Becca and I know. The girl's face is bruised and she walks stiffly like she's got other sore places on her body. She's got a beige scarf wrapped around her head like a turban. Her jeans are well worn and her navy T-shirt is ragged around the hem.

"It's Joy." Becca leads the girl to the table. "Here, you take this chair. I'll get another one."

Marilee and I look at each other and then look away. Joy's skin has that tired look that comes with cancer. I'd guess Becca was right when she said Joy is less than eighteen years old, too.

"Maybe you should start with something hot," Randy says to Joy as he gets up. "I've got some red pepper tomato soup. You can eat that while you decide what else to have. It's got lots of vitamin C."

"I don't need more than that," Joy says as she sets down the menu.

"You'll hurt Randy's feelings if you don't try a hamburger at least," Marilee says.

"You've got that right," Randy says as he turns to flash Joy a smile and heads to the kitchen.

"A hamburger does sound good," Joy says.

"You may as well have the works on it," Becca adds as she pulls her chair into the circle. "Extra cheese at least."

When Randy brings the platter out, Joy not only has extra cheese she also has a side salad with lots of tomato and avocado on it. I also see grilled onions for her burger and several sections of fresh-cut orange.

When Joy sees the platter of food, her face changes and I see the closest thing to what Mary might have looked like that I have seen all day. It's a brief flash of raw wonder followed by hesitation.

The waitress set everyone's platters down shortly after Randy brought Joy's to her, but I think we're all watching Joy while trying to look like we're not. I know I can't take my eyes off of her.

"It's too much. I didn't expect all this," Joy says quietly. "I can't pay for it."

"There's no charge," Randy says and then smiles at her. "I'm just testing out some new menu items and I thought you might give us your opinion."

A look of hope builds on Joy's face. "Well, if you're sure it's okay."

"It's definitely okay," Randy says quietly. "We need more customer feedback."

"Then I need to wash my hands first." Joy looks around.

"The hallway to the right of the counter." Randy points to the restrooms.

Jay stands up and walks to the hallway.

I sit there and think that maybe part of the holy wonder Mary felt was about hunger. I can only believe that when that angel talked to her, Mary wanted the angel's promise to come true with a hunger that has something in common with what Joy felt.

I half expected the initial rush of wonder. What I didn't think about was the hesitation that must have followed for Mary and then the sense that she wasn't good enough but was filled with hope anyway.

"You did a good thing with that hamburger platter you made for Joy," Quinn finally says to Randy.

"I packed it with as much nutrition as I could."

"I'm sure she'll eat as much as she can."

"She should really come in for eggs in the morning," Randy adds and then looks at me. "She's sick, isn't she?"

"I think so." Maybe those of us in the Sisterhood aren't the only ones who recognize the differences in skin color.

"There's got to be some agency that takes in sick people when they're homeless," Randy says as he stands up. "I know a guy who runs a nonprofit for kids on the street in Hollywood. I'm going to call him right now and see what we can do."

"He's a good guy," Becca says as Randy goes into the kitchen with his cell phone in his hand.

"Seems to be," Quinn says and I hear the hesitation in his voice so I know he's thinking, like the others might be thinking, about that offer of an apartment.

"Randy seems to worry about homeless women," I say just to give myself a minute to think of the words to say. Nothing fancy comes to me so I just say it. "I think he was worried about me and that's why he offered me a place to stay. I don't think he had any other motive."

"You?" Marilee says with a laugh. "You've got that big house. He doesn't need to worry about a place for you."

"The house belongs to my uncle," I say and then I admit what I haven't told anyone except Randy. "And I'm worried my uncle's going to tell me and my parents to leave. If he did, we'd have to scramble to find a place."

"But you're rich," Marilee protests.

I shake my head and look down. "My uncle supports us. Neither of my parents have worked in years. I plan to get a job soon, but my mother gets upset if I even talk about a regular job. She doesn't think any job is good enough for me. I'm going to have to do it eventually, but I want to wait until my dad gets back from his time in rehab. He's doing so good he might be able to get a job this time. My mother might not be so upset then."

I say it all in a rush and I know it comes out sounding jumbled. And maybe a little defensive.

There's silence for a minute and then Joy comes

back to the table. Just seeing Joy's legs come into view gives me the courage to lift my head. I look around the table at my friends. Marilee and Lizabett are both looking stunned. I can see Becca starting to form a question in her mind. Only Quinn seems to be at ease.

"You were worried about all that and you didn't tell us?" Becca finally gets her words out.

"We didn't have any rules about keeping secrets," Marilee says a little too quickly.

She's right; we didn't have a rule like that. But she knew, like I did, that everyone else had shared their lives. Marilee talked about the problems she'd had adjusting to her parents' divorce. Lizabett talked about how she felt her family was smothering her. Becca talked about the struggles she had trying to be her own person in her family. And, all that time, I let them believe my family life was as smooth and unruffled as they pictured it.

"How long have you been worried like this?" Becca ignores Marilee and demands to know.

"We've lived with my uncle since I was twelve. It's been okay," I say and then I stop myself. If I'm going to do this, I need to be honest. "I've been worried he's going to ask us to leave for the last six years or so."

"Since before you got your diagnosis?" Lizabett says softly as she scoots her chair a little closer to me and puts her hand on my shoulder.

I shake my head. "I started to worry about it *after* I heard about the Hodgkin's."

That was part of the reason I never said anything to anyone. I had so much to worry about with the cancer that I thought I was just imagining that my uncle didn't seem as tolerant of us being in his house.

"And you didn't say a word to us?" Becca asks. "I told you everything."

"We don't have any rules," Marilee stubbornly repeats what she said earlier.

By now, Joy has stopped eating and Quinn is looking at us all. I wouldn't be surprised if the people at the counter are paying close attention to us as well. There's enough tightly controlled emotion in Becca's voice to make anyone want to look over here or, if not that, to at least get ready to duck and cover from where they sit.

"I'm sorry," I finally say. "I just didn't know how to tell you."

My words hang there as the Sisterhood seems to absorb them. Finally, I hear footsteps and look over to see Randy coming back to the table.

"Good news," Randy says as he sits down. He looks at Joy. "I've got a place for you to stay for a few days. There's a place called—" Randy stops and looks around. "Did I miss something?"

"Carly just told us that she's worried that she and her parents might not be able to keep living with her uncle," Marilee says quietly.

"Yeah, that's why I mentioned the apartment over my diner. I can't rent it to anyone because my customers make so much noise when they're watching their sports games on television. But, if Carly didn't mind that, she could stay there for a while. Her parents, too, if they need to."

Becca looks at Randy. "She told you she was worried about the deal with her uncle?"

Randy nods and looks around in bewilderment.

"They're just upset that it took me a long time to tell them," I say.

In all the years I've been meeting with the Sisterhood, I've never disappointed them like this. Until it happened, I would have said I was so used to living with my mother's disappointment that I could deal with anyone else's as well. I would have been wrong to think that. I might not be so worried about cancer anymore, but the Sisterhood is still my lifeline.

Chapter Six

"A half-truth is a whole lie."

—*Jewish proverb*

Becca brought us this proverb to our meeting one night in the spring of the first year. We'd been talking about whether we wanted our doctors to tell us the whole truth or if we wanted them to hedge a little so we'd have more hope. Becca wanted her doctor to hit her with everything straight on. Kaboom. She wanted it all. I said I would rather my doctor not tell me anything if he couldn't give me some hope along with it. Becca and I were different even back then.

Becca respects the truth and that's why she'll make a good judge someday. I remind myself of that on Monday morning when I'm sitting in my advanced literature class. Dealing with things straight on is who Becca is. I should have known she would be the most upset.

Lizabett gave me a hug before I left The Pews yesterday and I know she doesn't have any hard feelings. Lizabett knows how difficult it is to get things said sometimes. Even Marilee recovered from the surprise of what I told everyone and managed to look me in the eye before we left.

But Becca was still just-under-the-surface angry. I know she didn't want to make me feel bad, but she barely managed to say goodbye before she left to drive Joy down to the place Randy had found.

Once Becca and Joy left The Pews yesterday, we all went home. I felt like I used to back in the days when I'd spend all day with doctors then come home tired. I crawled into bed early and I still felt weary when I got up this morning. Fortunately, I had my class so I made myself get dressed and leave the house.

My class ends before Lizabett's psychology class does so I take the bus down Colorado to wait at The Pews for her. It's one of our days for eating lunch together. It's nice to have these times to count on.

Marilee is already at The Pews working on the diner's books and ordering supplies for the week so she'll probably come to our room at noon. Lizabett should be there by then as well. I doubt Becca will come. She usually has a meeting with the judge late mornings on Mondays and so she just takes a sandwich with her for lunch. Of course, now she probably wouldn't come even if she didn't have a meeting.

I sit down in the room and close the French doors. Lizabett left some of the Mary books on the shelf we have and so I pull one off.

I keep thinking about secrets as I leaf through the book. I can't help but think about all the nights we met in this room behind these French doors. These doors have become symbolic to me in a way they wouldn't be to any of the others. When I kept my secrets, it was like I was always behind another set of invisible French doors. I could see everything that was happening in the Sisterhood, but I didn't feel like I was fully there when it happened.

I wish I had done it differently.

Secrets make a person cautious. That's one of the reasons I hesitated about writing in the journal, which is still sitting on the shelf where I left it, by the way. When a person has secrets, they are always worried about saying something that would give it all away.

This whole business about my uncle's house didn't seem like such a big secret initially. When the Sisterhood first met and we introduced ourselves, everyone told a little about their family and where they lived. I didn't even know Becca, Lizabett and Marilee back then. I didn't think there was any need for them to know the inside, messy business of my family. I only said I lived in San Marino with my parents. I never said we were rich or that my parents owned a house or anything.

I should have told them how it was at some point though. I thought about it when Marilee's parents separated. But when Marilee told us about her parents' divorce, something concrete had happened. Her father had left the house. I didn't have anything but my suspicions and my worries to go on. How could I take up Sisterhood time with my vague worries when Marilee was facing the real thing? If my uncle had actually told us to leave his house, then I am sure I would have said something.

I hear a knock on the French doors and I look up to see Randy.

"Want some company?" he asks as he opens the door.

"Please."

"I didn't mean to bring up the whole house thing yesterday," Randy says as he stands inside the door. He's got a white chef's apron on with a Lakers T-shirt beneath it.

He looks a little rumpled like he didn't sleep well either and I like that.

"It's not your fault," I say. "I should have told everyone a long time ago."

Randy walks over and sits down in a chair at the table. "I'm glad you told me."

"You're a good listener."

Randy shrugs. "The offer of that apartment still holds."

I nod. "I appreciate it."

There's another knock on the glass panes of the

French doors and Lizabett is standing there. I motion for her to come inside.

"How do you feel?" Lizabett says when she steps into the room.

"I'm fine," I say and then realize I need to keep being honest. "A little tired and worried about me and Becca, though."

"She'll be fine," Lizabett says. "She doesn't stay mad for long."

"She's right though, I should have told everyone."

Lizabett shrugs. "Sometimes it's hard to get all the words said when we're meeting. If you had thought you needed to tell us, you would have."

We're all silent for a moment.

Randy leaves to go back to the kitchen and Lizabett and I sit down with the Mary books. I have my first rehearsal this afternoon. The lead actors aren't going to be there so I'm sure I'll have some standing in place to do.

"I wonder when Mary learned to ride a donkey," Lizabett says as she looks at a picture in the book.

"I suppose it'd be like learning to ride a bicycle today," I say. "They probably learned when they were big enough to sit on the animal without falling off. Some neighborhood kid would come by and ask, 'Want to ride my new donkey?' and off they'd go."

One good thing about having the nativity play happening in the Depression is that there wouldn't have been many people riding donkeys in that time frame. Mary probably would be riding a bicycle instead. Or maybe riding in a beat-up old truck.

"I'm more curious about whether or not she had any friends," I say as I reach up and pull another book off the shelf. "And, if she had any friends, I wonder if she told any of them about the angel visit."

Lizabett can see where I'm going and she grins. "Becca would really be steamed if you kept something like that from her."

I nod. "Not all secrets are equal."

"The important thing is that you told us now."

"And no angel's been to visit me, so at least you know it's my biggest secret," I add.

"Mary must not have had any friends," Lizabett says. "It says that she didn't tell anyone about the angel visit and, if she had friends, they would have wanted to know. Besides, when she became pregnant—"

I nod. "Definitely no close friends. They would have been all over that. Especially the miracle part of the pregnancy."

I know many things had to have been different when Mary was growing up.

"Maybe teenagers didn't have friends like they do today," I say. It makes me feel a little sad for Mary if that were true. "I mean with all of the talking back and forth. I wouldn't like that."

"Me neither." Lizabett is leafing through a book. "She did have an aunt or a cousin or someone she went to visit, though."

"I can't imagine telling my aunt something like that." I shudder just thinking about it. My aunt gets fussy enough about mortal visitors that come to her door and ask for me. She wouldn't know what to do if an angel knocked.

Marilee comes into the Sisterhood room with several plastic containers filled with salad. "There was a pick-up order that got mixed up. So we have leftover salads. Want one?"

"Sure," Lizabett and I both say.

I watch Marilee carefully as she comes in the door and sits down. She doesn't seem any different today so she must be okay with me.

"I'm sorry about yesterday," I say, just to be sure. "Well, not just yesterday but for not telling you how it was in the first place years ago."

"Don't worry about it," Marilee says as she sets the salads on the table. "We're the Sisterhood. We make it through hard patches in life. That's what we do. We'll make it through this one."

I want to believe Marilee so I do.

"Becca's probably going to call any minute now and say she's not mad anymore," Lizabett says as she pulls one of the salad containers toward her.

"She was probably more hurt than mad anyway," Marilee says as she hands Lizabett a plastic fork and then holds one out to me. "When Becca realizes that, she'll call."

"I hope so." I take the fork and pull a salad container toward me. It's a Greek salad and I note there are a few black olives in it. Everything seems to remind me of Mary and the part of the world where she lived. It would be odd to have all the olives you wanted to eat but no cell phone to call your friends.

We talk about the play while we eat our salads.

This time Lizabett wants to come with me to my rehearsal and I say I think it will be okay. The play is being held in a huge church and we were already told they're not closing the doors during rehearsals, because people might want to come inside and pray. I told Lizabett that if she wants to bring one of her schoolbooks and study, I'd appreciate having someone there with me. She might even take some time to write in the Sisterhood journal.

Hi, this is Lizabett. Carly is right that we haven't been writing in the journal like we should. I'm sitting in the church where Carly is rehearsing so I thought I'd write a little about it. Carly is so totally cool when she's onstage. Honestly, I could see her being a Jennifer Aniston or someone. Not that the director seems too happy with her. He's not even looking at her. He just yells out directions to stand there or walk around that circle. I think they are trying to measure the road Joseph and Mary would have taken to Bethlehem. I wonder how long a pregnant woman can ride on a donkey.

I don't know what they're going to use instead of a donkey, but it's something with wheels because the director is using a stick to plot out turns. Every time the director makes a turn, Mary needs to stand in a new place so someone can measure everything.

I hope Carly gets a chance to be onstage as Mary.

There is an area where some of the cast members are getting their costumes while the director blocks out the action. There's a lot of faded material in the costumes. I see one man who is going to be a shepherd. He has a faded blue shirt and old denim jeans. I think he's a farmworker in the play rather than a nomadic shepherd like Mary might have known. Whoever he is, his straw hat is stained and frayed.

They also have some guys dressed up like '50s rock stars. I think they might represent the three wise men. They definitely have enough shiny gold necklaces and watches to be rich. They even have gold belts. Not that they're perfect. I don't see how they'd be able to see the night star with those dark sunglasses they are wearing..

I keep my eye out for the woman who is playing Mary, but she's not here today.

Ah, there's Carly walking again. She does everything just like the director asks her to and I think she does it with feeling. It's not easy to portray *I am the mother of the baby Jesus* just by the way you walk.

I really think this could be Carly's big break. I know this is a small experimental play, but people will be watching. After Carly said she's going to need to get a job before too long, I've been hoping that she will get some notice in this play. If she has to get a job, she won't be able to go to auditions and things like that. I wouldn't want her to miss her chance at stardom just because she has to get a job.

I know Carly says stars don't get discovered anymore, but this is a nativity play. Maybe there will be a miracle or two. I haven't said anything, but I've started to pray that Carly will get to actually be seen in this play. I'm not sure about prayer. Usually, I would just ask Quinn to pray for me, but I want to do this one on my own. I'm not sure God will listen to me, but I'm going for it.

Here Carly comes. They're taking a break. I notice Carly walks up the aisle toward me with dignity. She's a natural for the role of Mary.

I'll give the journal back to her now. I wonder if the reason I'm so determined to see Carly have some stage time is because she seems so upset about Becca. It's hard to tell because when Carly is upset she becomes even more poised than usual. But, when I look in her eyes, I can see she's hurt.

When I think about it, the Sisterhood should have paid more attention to Carly. We should have known that she was worried about something besides her cancer. Maybe Carly should be mad at us instead of Becca being mad at her.

If you're reading this, Carly, I want to say I'm sorry I didn't notice before that you were upset when you mentioned your family. You've certainly stood by me. I'll stand by you no matter what. Just tell us next time and we'll be there.

Chapter Seven

"Inside myself is a place where I live all alone and that's where you renew your springs that never dry up."

—*Pearl S. Buck*

Our counselor, Rose, brought this quote to the Sisterhood one evening when most of us were about halfway through our chemo and we were so very tired of everything. We all tried to figure out if we had a private place like the one Pearl S. Buck mentioned where we could go to renew ourselves. Lizabett said she had too many brothers to ever have to worry about being really alone. Rose said she thought the place was more mental than physical. Becca said her mind was too busy for a place like that. Only Marilee and I seemed to have any sense within ourselves that we had a place like Pearl Buck mentioned. Not that my place was

very refreshing. Some days it felt like it drained me more than it renewed me.

This is Carly. I've been to several rehearsals for the play and I'm looking forward to seeing it on the stage. I've seen how hard the cast members are working on their roles and I've decided I'm proud to be part of the cast even if I never set foot on the stage when there's an audience in front of it.

This play made me think of that quote Rose brought to us. Something about the nativity story reminds me of the place of renewing that Rose was talking about. I started to read the New Testament last night so I know more about Mary than I did even after reading the other books.

Mary seems like a person with a quiet place inside of her. The Bible says she kept the things the angel told her in her heart. The place in Mary's heart sounds like it was a warm and secure place like the one Rose was describing. I wonder if Marilee has a place like that in her heart now that she's going to church.

It's Wednesday morning and I'm sitting in class again. I'm having a hard time paying attention to the professor. I haven't talked to Becca since Sunday, but I know she's busy with her internship. It's not unusual for her to go for a few days, or even all week, without talking to me. I left a message on her phone yesterday and she hasn't responded. Ordinarily, she would have at least talked to one of us

in the Sisterhood, but neither Marilee nor Lizabett have made any mention of calls they have received from her. No one has even mentioned an e-mail.

The professor assigns us a report to be written on a book from a different culture. We're supposed to read the book and compare the culture we find in the book with our own. I wonder if the nativity story from the Bible would count. They certainly had a different culture back then. And since people are still making play adaptations from the Bible, the professor would have to classify it as literature.

Speaking of the play, I've heard rumors from the other cast members that a couple of big television producers are going to be watching on opening night. One's working on a new prime-time comedy and the other is putting together a reality show. I knew when I heard those rumors that there would be no way the actress playing Mary would get sick and let her understudy go on. She would be there if she had to hide a broken leg under that long gown she's going to be wearing.

I had to stand for the costume fitting so I know a person could hide a full plaster cast under the dress the wardrobe person is putting together. It's all Depression-era clothing and I'm not sure anyone had stylish maternity clothes back then. Mostly it seems they just made tents and draped it over the woman. I guess if you were pregnant you wouldn't be going any place fancy back then anyway.

The dress the costume designer made looked like

it was made from old flour sacks. She was telling me that people really did make clothes out of the flour sacks and that the flour people obliged by printing tiny little flowers on some of the sacks. The dress for Mary had bluebells stamped on it. I think Mary would have liked bluebells.

I had a pillow strapped to me while the costume designer fitted the dress, so it's not like the dress is any more stylish than other clothes of the era or anything. It's made of coarse cotton and it scratches. Still, I have to admit I would like to wear the costume and be in the play instead of just standing on the sidelines.

I know a lot of people have to spend time on the sidelines. I'm not complaining; I've had more than my share of the spotlight over the years. I'm beginning to think though that I would trade a chance to walk across that stage as Mary for that time I was the Rose Parade Queen.

There's just something about Mary that draws me to her.

I mean it when I tell Lizabett that it would be an honor to represent Mary in the play. Enough time has passed so that both Lizabett and I have taken a bus down to The Pews. We're sitting at our table with some of Quinn's books spread out around us.

"You should learn the lines so you can say them, just in case," Lizabett says. "I have a feeling that this could be your special break. Especially with those producers coming."

"Of course I'm going to learn the lines," I say. I frown as I think about it. "It's odd that the director hasn't asked me to learn the lines already. Shouldn't he do that?"

Lizabett shrugs. "Maybe he's getting to it."

"There's not that much time until opening night." The more I think about it the more I wonder. "Maybe I should ask him."

Randy brings in a couple of bowls of soup and two just-ripened imported pears for us. The pears are all cut up on a plate with a few small slices of imported cheese.

Lizabett watches the tray as Randy sets it in on the table. "Wow."

"I don't usually see fruit like this at Uncle Lou's," I say. "Thank you. Is this part of the menu change thing?"

Randy shakes his head. "No, it's just for you. You mentioned your mother buys the fancy fruit."

I look at Randy. "I'm very impressed."

Randy looks pleased. "If you need anything more, let me know."

Then he leaves the room.

"Wow," Lizabett repeats as she turns to me. "I've never had a guy buy me an imported piece of fruit before."

I shake my head. "He didn't need to do that."

"But he did," Lizabett says as she reaches for a piece of a pear.

We eat every single piece of pear and cheese on

the plate and then Lizabett goes off to make a phone call as I turn my attention back to the journal.

I'm picking up where I left off. Well, maybe not right where I left off as I have something else I want to say. It's about the pear. I think there's something twisted about me. Not twisted in a horror movie kind of a way, but in the different-than-what-most-people-are kind of way. I'm thinking just the opposite of what Lizabett is about that pear.

So Randy brings me an imported pear, cut into perfect little wedges. What could be wrong with that? A few months ago, I would have said there was absolutely nothing wrong. But I'm not so sure anymore. My mother has given me imported fruit for years now and all it has done is make me feel I need to keep silent about who I really am. I'm not some princess who can't be happy with a regular pear. I don't want Randy to treat me like that.

In San Marino I see a fair number of women who fit the stereotype of trophy wives. They look sleek and expensively dressed. We're talking really expensive here. They spend their days at the gym or the spa. They don't have jobs, but everything they want is given to them anyway. They take it as their right to be served imported fruit on a dainty platter without even needing to worry about who's going to wash the platter after they finish with it.

I'm not saying that all women in San Marino are

like that. Or even that most of the women are. But my aunt and her friends are. My mother tries to be.

If Randy wants to put me on some princess pedestal, we are going to have problems. It's not just the pear, either. It's also the apartment. I don't think he has an ulterior motive in offering me the apartment, but I'm not going to ever be a grown-up if I don't learn to take care of myself.

I feel as though I'm one of those glass ornaments my mother collects for Christmas, something packed in tissue paper and only brought out on special occasions.

I want to live a life with more mess in it. Even Mary wasn't carried along on some feather pillow; she had to ride that donkey and it couldn't have been too comfortable.

I look at my watch and see I need to sign off now. I promised Lizabett I would meet her back here after the rehearsal session this afternoon. She is going to her ballet class right now. If she wasn't, she'd probably want to come with me and watch this rehearsal as well. Oh, well, I'll tell her all about it when I see her later. I expect the director will have some new poses for me today.

I don't get back to The Pews until dark. My body hurts in places I didn't know I had. The director wanted me to ride in the back of the old pickup to see if the actress playing Mary would be okay when she did it. The director wanted Mary and Joseph to be in the back of the pickup so the audience could hear the two of them making comments as they drove down the dusty old road. Besides, he had some great special effects going in the background that made one scene look like a thunderstorm.

I'm beginning to think Mary knew what she was doing when she rode on the donkey. Any animal would have a smoother gait than an old diesel pickup.

I met the woman who is playing Mary today. She came by when I had finished the test run in the pickup.

"At least you won't have to ride in that pickup in front of an audience," she said after she'd told me she was playing Mary. I could tell she was sizing me up and she looked a little worried about what she saw. I recognized the signs from my Rose Queen days.

"I know," I assured her. "The director already told me not to expect to go on. Don't worry."

She nodded in relief. "It's just that there's going to be a producer from the new reality show coming to one of the performances. I don't know which performance he's coming to, so I won't be missing any of them."

"I had heard there were going to be some producers showing up."

The woman had chin-length black hair and a tattoo of a butterfly on her hand. She used her hands a lot when she talked.

"I'm a nervous wreck. I'm trying so hard to make a go of this acting thing. It could be my big break if a producer notices me. I'm not sure I'd fit the comedy thing, but I'm hoping for the reality show—it's filming in Cancún, Mexico, you know. In the meantime, I'm taking every little show I can find." She started to thaw even more as she talked. "My boyfriend and I are both performing in a couple of shows right now. He's Joseph in this one."

"That's great that you can work together."

The woman leaned in toward me to speak low and confidential. "It really works well because our other show is up at Big Bear. I wouldn't want to drive those mountain roads by myself this time of year. We do a morning rehearsal up there and have just enough time to get back for our rehearsal here."

I nodded. I wouldn't want to drive those roads in the winter either. The town of Big Bear is in the San Bernardino Mountains, about an hour and a half east of Pasadena. It's the place everyone goes for skiing, but it has a good sized theatre community as well.

The woman took a deep breath and continued. "I know you probably want to get seen by a producer, too, but—"

I assured the woman again that the director had told me I wouldn't be seeing any time on the stage. Which made her feel good, but, after she walked away, I began to wonder why the director had hired me to be the understudy in the first place. My height and build didn't match hers at all. Surely, there was someone else in that line at the auditions that would have been a better match.

I got the answer to my question after rehearsal

that day. The director asked to talk with me a minute. It turns out he recognized my home address from the forms I filled out. He knows my uncle and was hoping my uncle would allow the cast to have an opening night party at his house.

"I know Harold and Susan," the director said. That's my aunt and uncle. "I've seen them at charity events over the years. But, since you live with them, I'm hoping you might put in a good word. You've probably heard there's going to be some big Hollywood names here for our opening night and a good party sets the tone for getting some media buzz. You know how it is. We have family financing for this production, but we're hoping to get the real thing for next year."

"Oh," I said, trying to think of a way to tell the director that I didn't have any influence with my uncle unless we counted the fact that he might be worried he'd look bad if he refused to hold the party. Or cheap, which would have been worse in my uncle's opinion.

"Oh, gotta go," the director said as he looked over my head at something else. "I had my assistant call your uncle today, so if you get a chance to mention it to him again that'd be great. I want him to know it's the play you're working on."

The director left before I could say anything else.

The woman who is playing Mary walked back over to me. "I thought you said you weren't going onstage at all."

"That's what he told me," I said even though the woman kept looking at me suspiciously.

"But he knows your uncle."

"Believe me, that's not going to make a difference. Honest."

I smiled at her to be reassuring. She walked away and that was that. I hope she doesn't stay up nights worrying about something that isn't going to happen.

Lizabett and Marilee are both waiting for me when I get back to The Pews.

"What's wrong?" Marilee says as I limp into the room.

"Where do I begin?" I manage to make it to a chair. "I had to try out the back of the pickup so Mary wouldn't be bumped around too much as she and Joseph hitch a ride to Bethlehem. It's on account of her being pregnant. The director doesn't want her to be jostled too much."

Marilee looks at me. "Is the actress who's playing Mary pregnant?"

"I don't think so. She's rehearsing another play up in Big Bear."

"Then why do you have to be bumped around so she isn't?"

"Because I'm the understudy."

I know it sounds strange, but I don't mind being the one who makes the ride easy for the princess for a change. I think a lot of that is because I picture the real Mary in the role in the play and I don't mind making the road easy for her.

"Well, I don't think it's fair," Lizabett says. "You might be the understudy, but you're every bit as good of an actress as the one who's going to play the part."

I smile at Lizabett's fierce loyalty. "I met the woman who's playing Mary today. She's got this butterfly tattoo on the back of her hand."

"I bet she was nervous that you'll take over," Lizabett says.

"Only because she heard that the director wants to have an opening night party at my uncle's house in San Marino."

"What?" Marilee says.

"Your uncle's house?" Lizabett echoes.

"Is that okay?" Marilee asks.

I shrug. "The director said he'd already called and left a message, so it's too late to do anything about it now. Besides, once I realized my aunt would get the message instead of my uncle, I figured it was already a done deal. If I know my aunt, she's already called the director back and agreed to it. She'll brag for weeks if she can have a few Hollywood producers in her living room. She likes any kind of celebrities."

Actually, my uncle has three living rooms, but who's counting? The house has a formal living room, a semiformal living room and then a not-quite-casual living room. They all connect together with huge sliding doors that can be opened to make a party area for a couple of hundred guests. With all of the Christmas decorations that are up, it would be a great place for an opening-night party.

"But what about your uncle?" Marilee asks. "Your aunt's got to tell him. Is this good or bad for all of you and him?"

"I don't know. I just hope he doesn't do it because he feels trapped. He wouldn't want to look like an uncaring uncle in front of any Hollywood people."

"If there's anything we can do, let us know," Lizabett says.

"Yeah, we can pass crackers or cut up fruit or anything like that," Marilee adds.

"It won't be anything that simple if my aunt and important people are involved," I say. Just thinking about it all makes my bones ache even more. "But I'll be grateful for your help."

Usually, when my aunt has a party, my parents and I stay up in our rooms. Since I'm part of the play, however, my aunt will probably think we need to be there passing around appetizers or something.

"It won't be anything the Sisterhood can't handle," Marilee says, and then stops. "Oh."

I nod. "We could use Becca's help. I hope she's talking to me by then."

"Oh, she will be," Lizabett says.

I go home that night and soak in the tub. I don't knock on the main door to talk to my aunt or uncle. I decide that the morning is soon enough for that.

I drift off to sleep reminding myself that I was the one who wanted to stop being treated like a princess. A few sores from honest work are a good step in that direction. I am getting paid for my understudy role, I remind myself. It'll be almost five hundred dollars total and I'm going to start my move-out fund with it. I already have a thousand or so in my savings account. My dad will be home before I know it and then it will be time for me to get a place of my own.

I'm a little scared, but also excited about the future. The Mary of the Bible could do the things that lie ahead of me and so can I. That reminds me, I meant to ask Marilee if the church where she is going has any books about Mary. Even if it's only for my practice sessions in The Pews, I want to get the role of Mary absolutely right.

Chapter Eight

"A diamond with a flaw is worth more than a pebble without imperfections."

—*Chinese proverb*

Becca brought this quote to the Sisterhood one year in the month of June. We were all watching a few of our classmates get engaged and diamonds were the big thing. We tried not to be envious, but we weren't too successful at it. None of us were even dating. Getting through our chemo was all we could do; we had no energy for going out on dates. We even had to decline half of the wedding invitations we received because of our health. I remember thinking at the time that Becca took it the hardest. She wanted to keep pounding ahead with her life and her body was betraying her with its weakness. She truly believed that if she didn't give in, she could do anything.

* * *

I miss Becca. This is Carly, and it's already Thursday morning. We have our Sisterhood meeting tonight and I'm worried Becca won't even come. We've all missed Sisterhood meetings here and there, but I don't think anyone has ever deliberately stayed away because she was upset with someone else.

Of course, that's probably because Becca wouldn't let any of the rest of us stay away. She would insist the angry person talk to everyone until the feelings were handled and everyone was happy again. The problem is that Becca is the one who is gone. Who's going to go and talk to her?

I've been spending a lot of time at The Pews and, when Lizabett can't help me, Randy has been helping me learn the role of Mary. He reads me the words of Joseph so I can practice Mary's responses.

We're doing that now.

"I love only you," I say as I lean into Randy. Well, I try to lean into him. That's what the script tells me to do, but the pillow I have tucked into my jacket makes me want to tip off the table rather than lean into Randy.

We are sitting on an edge of the table in our room at The Pews. I figure if I'm going to practice, I should practice as the pregnant woman I'd be if I ever had a chance to do the role in the play.

"I trust you," Randy says as he takes hold of my

arm to steady me. He's reading from the same script that I am. "We won't be long now."

Randy bends down and gives me a kiss on the forehead. That's in the script, by the way.

We let a minute pass. I'm wondering if Mary was content with that forehead kiss. I'm thinking a real one would be nicer. Like the one Randy gave me the night he drove me home.

Instead, Mary has words to say. "Do you think there'll be work where we're going?"

"God will provide," Randy says as he puts his arm around me.

I have a denim jacket on so I'm a little warm when Randy puts his arm around me.

"I hope they have tomatoes there," I read from the script. "There's always work when there's tomatoes."

I look away from the script and up at Randy. "I hope no one thinks Mary is going to go picking tomatoes. I don't care what year this play is supposed to take place in."

The play has prompted me to do a lot of thinking about Mary, but it is, I think, an unusual kind of thinking.

"I guess that's creative license for you," Randy says. "I can't imagine Joseph would let Mary do something like that, though. A man should take care of his wife. If he has one, that is."

Randy clears his throat.

"Most women do some kind of work these days," I say as I look up into his eyes. Definitely slate-blue cool, but I keep going. "Maybe not picking tomatoes, but something."

Please have the right answer, I think.

Randy is looking back at me. "I know. That's the way it is." His voice gets a little funny and he smiles. "But my wife wouldn't need to work. I'll even have a maid to take care of the house. My wife will have time for whatever she wants to do."

"Like going to the spa and shopping," I say, looking back down at the script.

"Yeah, things like that," Randy says. "Fun stuff."

I notice he keeps his arm around me.

We keep going on with the script, but my mind stays back there with those tomatoes. It's not that I want to work like a farmworker every day of my life. But I do want to be able to take care of myself if I need to do so. Some women might want to make a career out of leisure, but I'm not one of them.

Besides, in my observation, a man whose wife does nothing productive expects her to impress people for him. Maybe that's her job: she's supposed to look like she's so rich she never needs to lift a finger and he's so rich he can afford to support her in that style.

I'm not interested in being a princess all of my life. My mother has cured me of that, if nothing else.

I can't help but wonder if Joseph treated Mary like a princess, though. He knew she was special, and not just special to him but to the whole world. If anyone deserved to be treated that way, it was Mary. From all I can tell, though, she lived her life rather humbly.

She didn't get one of those big blue stork signs to put on her lawn and announce to everyone that she'd given birth to the Messiah. She wasn't calling up the *National Enquirer.* She seemed to just let things flow along. If people came to see the baby, she welcomed them. But she didn't go passing Jesus around to strangers hoping to impress someone enough to get her on television or something.

I remember that the actress who is playing Mary just wants to get ahead and I think she's got the wrong idea. The role of Mary should be acted for the sheer honor of doing it, quietly and humbly and with no expectation of fame or fortune.

We finish going through the script when Marilee comes to the door.

"Guess what?" Marilee says as she comes into the room with a nod for Randy and me. "I just got an e-mail from Becca."

"Oh?" I say just like my heart isn't starting to pound. "Is she coming tonight?"

"She said she has to do something for Joy and that it is really important or she would be here."

"Oh." My heart isn't pounding so much anymore. "I see."

Randy puts his arm back around my shoulders and gives me a little squeeze.

"I'm sure she wants to be here," Marilee adds.

"Do you really think so?" I say as I look up at Marilee. I figure if I'm going to be more honest with the Sisterhood, it should operate both ways.

"I hope so," Marilee says softly.

I nod. "So do I."

"At least Rose will be here tonight," Marilee says.

Rose has been with us through thick and thin. She was our rock in the days when we were in treatment. She's out helping other teenagers now, so she doesn't get to our group as often as she did in the beginning, but she makes it about once a month. I'm glad she'll be here tonight.

Marilee goes back to her office and Randy goes to the kitchen to get ready for the dinner crowd. I sit in our room and work on my Mary list. At first, I thought I'd write out a description of Mary, but I never got organized enough to do that so I settled for making a list of observations I have made about her life after reading the books I've read.

My first observation is that Mary knew longing. Actually that is something I gathered from the part of the New Testament that I have read. There is an awful lot about longing in that book. Well, it's more a longing and completion cycle. There are the thirsty ones who get water and the hungry ones who get bread and the lonely ones who get visited. Everybody needs something they don't already have. Because of all that, I believe Mary was a girl who had dreams. She might even have had a longing for a husband and a son.

Knowing that Mary probably had those kinds of feelings makes her more real to me. Sometimes, when I read about Mary, I picture her as a teenager like I was, attending San Marino High School. She would be the shy one in the corner; the one who wanted to date the basketball star but who didn't have the courage to even say hello to him.

I hope Joseph was Mary's basketball star. That she found in him all she hoped for in a husband.

With all of my reading in the New Testament, I'm becoming more curious about churches. I'm debating about asking Marilee if I can go to church with her and Quinn this Sunday. Marilee talks about that place enough that she shouldn't be surprised that I'd like to go with her.

I do some homework while I wait for the Sisterhood meeting to begin. I watch the dinner crowd come into The Pews. I've grown to love looking through the glass panes in these French doors. I try to imagine what the story is with different people who are on the other side having dinner. Sometimes you will see two friends laughing about something, but you can also see couples who are obviously arguing. It's hard to guess who's happier, though. Maybe the laughter hides tears and the anger will soon be turned to joy.

I guess in life a person just never knows. If you had asked me a month ago what my life would be now, I never would have guessed I would have developed a fondness for the Mary of the Bible and that I would have angered Becca so that she's not talking to me.

I get the room ready for the Sisterhood meeting

after I eat a sandwich out front. I don't usually spend the whole afternoon here, but I am avoiding my aunt and uncle. I decided I would leave them a note before I left this morning telling them that the director of the play had told me that he was asking them to host a cast party for the play I was in, but that they should feel under no obligation to do so. I assured them that I didn't expect anything like that and that the director could find another place for the party.

Communicating through notes is not unusual with me and my aunt and uncle. My aunt has a heavy silver tray that she leaves on a table just inside the front door for mail and notes like that. The housekeeper will take the tray and deliver whatever is on it to my aunt. I think my aunt likes to be served with that silver tray. It must make her feel like the queen of something.

Anyway, when I get home after the Sisterhood meeting, there will probably be an envelope in the old mailbox on the side of the house by the entrance my parents and I use. My aunt is always good about responding to notes.

I arrange the table and chairs the way we usually have them for the Sisterhood meetings. Randy and I had moved some things around earlier to make our stage, so I am careful to have everything in its proper place.

I brought the red silk yarn with me so I can begin making a scarf with it. I already have most of my

Christmas presents purchased, so I don't know who I am making the scarf for. I guess I'll knit it and see who comes to mind.

Lizabett is the first one to get here for the Sisterhood. Her hair is wet when she comes in and she shakes herself.

"Rain," she says. "And I didn't have an umbrella with me."

"Let me go get some paper towels for you."

I go to the kitchen and get a roll of paper towels. If Lizabett is wet, the others might be, too. I can hear the sound of the rain on the roof when I am in the kitchen of The Pews.

"Don't let me forget to give all of you your tea," Randy calls over to me from the grill. "Uncle Lou gave me strict instructions on that before he left. I don't think he would have gone to Italy if he thought I was forgetting your tea, especially when it's raining outside like this."

"Uncle Lou swears his tea is what got us through our treatments," I say. "And maybe he's right."

Not that I think the tea made such a difference, but having Uncle Lou faithfully bring it to us did make us feel better. I wonder as I go back to the room why I liked Uncle Lou's tea so much and didn't like the imported fruit Randy had brought in earlier. Is it just because the one is more common? When I get back to the room, Rose and Marilee are also there.

Rose is the only one who brings an umbrella with

her tonight. She comes into the room with her hair dry and her umbrella dripping. I wish you could see Rose. She is a medium height and a medium build. You wouldn't pick her out in a crowd unless you looked at her closely. But she has the kindest face of anyone I know. I can never decide if that's because her blue eyes are so expressive or because her smile is so genuine. Rose can laugh and cry with abandon. She's about fifty and she wears her dark hair in short curls around her head. She's not married and she never tells us if she goes on any dates.

"Sorry I'm late," Rose says as she sets her umbrella in a corner. "I got caught in traffic."

Because Rose continues to work as a counselor with teenagers who have cancer, many of her evenings are taken up with family therapy sessions. Rose pulls some yarn and knitting needles out of her big purse. "I've looked forward to this all day."

Rose is making an afghan for a cousin in North Dakota. She has relatives all over the Midwest and she's been knitting afghans for many of them. The afghan she's working on now is from a forest-green yarn.

We have a routine in our Sisterhood meetings. We knit in silence for the first half an hour and then we begin to talk. Usually, I find the first half hour very soothing, but not tonight. I keep looking up at the grandfather clock we have in the corner of the room. I can't quite wait for the full half hour to be up.

"Becca's mad at me," I finally say to Rose.

"Oh?" Rose says at the same time as Lizabett and Marilee protest that it's not so.

"I told her that my parents and I live with my uncle and that we have no money," I say. "Not that Becca cares about the money. She's mad because I let everyone believe something about me that isn't true."

I'm expecting Rose to be surprised.

"I was wondering when you were going to feel comfortable enough to tell everyone," Rose says calmly.

"You knew?"

Rose nods. "I had to have a meeting with your parents when you first started treatment. Your mother told me your financial situation."

"I never knew my parents met with you."

"All of the parents meet with me, at least initially. The hospital requires it."

I don't know if I am more surprised that my parents met with Rose without telling me or that they told her our family secrets when they did see her. All through school, my parents had avoided any parent-teacher conferences. I never thought they met with anyone about me.

I look around and Marilee and Lizabett are absorbing this news as well. I guess we were so totally focused on ourselves when we first started meeting with Rose that we never gave much thought to what she did in the official part of her job.

"I think Becca will come around before long,"

Rose says. "She just needs to work through this all in her own way."

"I didn't mean to let her down," I say.

Rose nods. "The Sisterhood is important to Becca. She'll work it through."

I hope Rose knows what she's talking about.

I knit some more on the red scarf I'm making. We talk about the play I'm in and Lizabett gives her impersonation of me bouncing along in the back of the old pickup during that one rehearsal. I laugh with the rest of them, thinking all the time that Lizabett should be the one onstage.

Randy brings in our cups of tea on a tray.

We decide not to meet next Thursday because it will be December 22, the opening night of the Mary play. I have enough tickets for all of the Sisterhood to come. The cast party that the director wants to host at my uncle's house is also that night.

"We don't need to be guests at the party," Marilee says. "I'm happy to serve or help or whatever."

"Thanks, I appreciate that. But be sure you plan to come."

If my aunt and uncle do go ahead with the party, I don't know how the food will go. Maybe the director will provide some. Maybe my aunt will hire a caterer. Maybe my aunt will want me and my friends to serve up appetizers we buy somewhere. It all depends on how socially important my aunt feels the party will be. If any kind of important people are going to be there, the food will be good.

Marilee drives me home and lets me out of her car at the front door of my uncle's house.

"I know you go to the side door," she says. "But the light is better here."

She looks at the side of the building. "I could walk with you though. It's pretty dark back there."

"You can come if you want," I say. "At least then you'll see what the note says from my aunt."

Marilee and I stand beside the side door and talk for a bit. There's enough light to read my aunt's note. She says she's delighted to host the party for their good friend, the director, and that she's excited about meeting the celebrities he will bring. She also says that she had no idea I was in a play and wasn't that exciting.

"I guess the director didn't bother to mention I'm the understudy and not really in the play," I say after I read the note. There's one more person to tell that it's unlikely I'll be onstage.

"Does it bother you? Being the understudy?" Marilee asks.

I shake my head. "Not anymore."

"Good."

Marilee and I hug good-night and I watch her as she walks back to her car.

I go to sleep easier tonight than I have in the past several nights. Maybe it's because I trust Rose when she says things will work out between Becca and me.

A friendship is a delicate thing. The ties in a family are stronger; a sister is a sister even if she's not talking to you. But a friend can become a non-friend just by declaring the friendship is over. It can happen so fast. Even a marriage requires a legal divorce to undo it. A friendship has no tie but the most voluntary one.

Chapter Nine

"In his later years, Pablo Picasso was not allowed to roam an art gallery unattended, for he had previously been discovered in the act of trying to improve on one of his old masterpieces."

—*Unknown*

Rose is the one that brought this quote to the Sisterhood during one of our difficult times. It really is more of a fact than a quote, but we loved it. We were all in chemo then and barely able to drag ourselves to the meetings. Rose brought the quote to us for a laugh, because she knew things like that delighted us.

After the laughter died away, Marilee asked if God, like Picasso, was trying to change us in some way after we were already supposed to be finished and that's why we had cancer. She always was the one who wanted to know why God had let this all happen to us. When we decided on our name, the Sisterhood of the Dropped Stitches, Marilee said it was a good fit because God had dropped some stitches when He made us.

Hi, this is Carly. It's Sunday morning and I'm going crazy. I made the mistake of telling my mother last night that Randy is taking me to church this morning. It's the church where Quinn and Marilee go so it's not a date, but try telling that to my mother. I'm taking a few minutes to sit on the balcony and have a glass of orange juice while I write a few notes in the journal. I told my mother I needed to prepare myself for church by coming out here. She looked a little confused, but at least she let me escape.

I'm wearing that old flannel robe, which doesn't make my mother happy, either. But my cat likes this robe and she followed me out here to cuddle in the hem that is lying at my feet. If my cat wasn't here with me, she'd be on my bed nesting so I let her stay.

My bed is covered with clothes. I will admit I am the one who started the pile and not my mother. I have no idea what to wear to a church service and that became apparent when I looked in my closet. I don't think I should wear anything flashy, but I don't want to go too casual, either. I want to show God I'm respectful and serious.

I'm not sure I'd be having any of this anxiety if

I hadn't been reading the New Testament lately. I've got to say that reading that book is changing my viewpoint about God. The truth is I'm beginning to think He might be real.

Yikes. I know.

That's why I'm having such a clothes crisis. Ordinarily, I'd pick something from my closet to wear that would be appreciated by the people who would see me in church. That's not so hard; I know how to dress to impress people. But I don't know how to dress to impress God.

I wonder if He likes wool suits.

Uh-oh, my mother is coming down the hall looking for me. I better get going.

I pick up my cat and step back into the hallway only to discover my mother is thinking of basic black. She's holding up the short dressy thing I wore for a reception during the Rose Queen competition. It was designed to win the votes of male judges.

"You can't go wrong with black," my mother says as she holds up the hanger.

The early-morning light filters into the hallway and there's enough sunlight to make the sequins on the dress sparkle. Not that there's a lot of sequins, but there's one single tasteful row of them outlining the neckline and it makes the dress shimmer.

"This is church, Mother. I don't think I should wear something that's low cut."

"But it's a church *date.* With your friend,

Randy. And, trust me, men have always liked this dress. I swear it's what got you the crown for the Rose Parade."

"I don't want to be overdressed."

"You don't want to be a wallflower, either." My mother purses her lips in the way she has that's supposed to tell me she expects me to be difficult so she's overlooking it this one time.

"I'm thinking maybe a black skirt and a plain white button-down blouse," I say.

My mother looks horrified. "People will think you're a waitress."

"That's fine. Being a waitress is good, honest work."

Mary might have even been a waitress if there had been restaurants back in Biblical times. Come to think of it, I wonder if there were restaurants then. It's odd to think of a place without any. Certainly, they would at least have had vendors along the roads like the hot dog stands they have at the beach today. People had to eat even if they were living in Biblical days.

"There's nothing wrong with some women being waitresses, but—" My mother narrows her eyes. "This Randy doesn't expect you to work for him if you get married, does he? I won't have you spending your life working in some man's diner. You were the Rose Queen, remember? You deserve better."

"Mother." I take a deep breath. I'll never forget I was the Rose Queen; my mother won't let me. "Randy and I haven't even gone out. I don't think you need to worry about anyone getting married quite yet. Besides—"

"Oh, I'm not opposed to you marrying the man. That diner of his is a good business. He gets big-name professional athletes there."

"Besides," I continue as though my mother hasn't spoken, "there is nothing wrong with any honest job. I don't want to spend my life as—" It suddenly strikes me what my mother just said. "How do you know so much about Randy's business?"

"Well, I called up that diner where you hang out and talked to him about it. He was really very nice. He seemed to understand that a mother would have concerns about her daughter. And he makes a very good income."

Okay. So now I'm thinking of wearing a bag over my head when I go to church. I gave my mother the telephone number to The Pews years ago and, to my knowledge, she's never used it until now. It was supposed to be for emergencies.

"Mother, we've never even gone out on a real date yet."

"And you never will if you wear a uniform. That's what a black skirt and a white blouse is. It's a uniform. It says *don't bother to look at me, I'm just here doing my job*."

"I hope nobody does look at me," I say as I walk back toward my room with my cat in my arms.

I let my cat down and she finds her bed in the corner of my room.

Then I look into my closet hoping there's something else in there that would work for church. I finally pull out a navy dress. It's fitted and has simple lines. I put it on and it looks nice and dignified.

I walk back out into the hallway. My mother is still there waiting for me to come out.

"Well," she says grudgingly. "I guess it's better than the skirt and blouse. You should let your hair down. You have such lovely blond hair. Randy will like that."

I have my hair pulled back into a bun at the back of my head. "I'm not worried about impressing Randy this morning."

"You're going to church," my mother says suspiciously. "Who else are you trying to impress?"

"God."

My mother thinks I'm being flip. I can see that right away.

"Seriously, Mom," I say as gently as I can. "That's why I'm going to church. I want to learn more about God."

"We've never had any problems with God in our family," my mother says defensively. "If you had questions, you should have come to your father and me."

"That's okay," I say. I can't even think of how to address that statement. My mother never mentions God, not even at Christmas.

"It's where Marilee goes to church now. It's a good church."

"Well, I hope Randy takes you out to lunch afterward," my mother says. "And not at that Pews place. You spend too much time there already. Make him take you to a nice restaurant. Maybe the brunch at the Ritz-Carlton. You've always liked the brunch there."

"I've only eaten there a few of times. You're the one who likes the brunch there."

"Well, what's not to like? They have lobster and shrimp. And eggs Benedict. And—"

"I know." I raise my hand. "They have everything."

I've taken my mother there for Mother's Day for the past few years. It's not the kind of place I'd like for a lunch with Randy. I'd like to just sit someplace and talk to him.

Just then the doorbell rings.

"That's him," I say as I give my mother a quick kiss on the cheek.

"Don't forget your jacket," my mother says. "It might rain."

I stop in my bedroom to get my jacket and my purse before I go down the stairs.

When I open the door for Randy, I see him look up the stairway behind me. He waves at someone and I look over my shoulder to see my mother beaming down upon us.

"Have fun," my mother calls down.

"We will, Mrs. Winston," Randy calls back. "Don't worry."

"She's going to worry anyway," I say as I close the door behind us.

"It's nice to have your mother interested in you," Randy says as we step off the small porch.

Dark gray clouds have started to move into the area since I was sitting out on the balcony earlier. We follow the sidewalk out to the street. The front lawn of my uncle's house is larger than some city parks. The grass is always green and trimmed to just the right length. The bushes are sculpted and the trees dignified. There are no swing sets or basketball hoops on the lawns of San Marino.

"I'm sorry she called you," I say as we reach the end of the walkway.

Randy's Jeep is at the curb. "I didn't want to pull in the driveway in case your uncle needed to get his car out."

"Thanks."

Randy opens the door to the passenger side of his Jeep. "And don't worry about your mother. She only wants you to be happy."

"Sometimes I wish she could want me to be happy from a little farther away," I say. "She treats me like I'm sixteen."

I step up into the Jeep and sit in the passenger seat.

Randy nods. "It's because of the cancer. She told me that."

Randy closes the door.

Whoa. I have to wait for Randy to walk around and open the driver's side door.

"You mean you actually had a *conversation* with my mother?"

I thought my mother had just asked Randy a few pointed questions. I had no idea they had actually talked.

Randy climbs into the driver's seat. "Well, sure. She told me how hard it was for her to accept that you had cancer and how she worried about you night and day because she didn't think you were taking it seriously enough."

Randy closes the door and starts the ignition.

"Not taking it seriously enough? I thought I was dying. I had these fevers and night sweats and—" I stop. "Besides, she didn't even want to admit that I had cancer. She told everyone I had mono."

Randy looks over at me and nods. "She said it was hard for her to accept."

I need to take a deep breath here so I wait for Randy to drive away from the curb. "I know my mother means well. I'm sure you understand how it is. Does your mother do this to you?"

Randy shakes his head as he turns onto a main street. "My mother died when I was eight."

"Oh, I'm sorry."

"That's okay. It's been a long time."

I'm silent for a minute. "You could share my mother. She can worry enough for two."

Randy chuckles. "Thanks."

Randy printed out the directions to the church we're going to from MapQuest and I give him the right and the left turns until we get there.

I'm still kind of spinning from this mother

business. I know I complain some about my mother. Okay, a lot. But I'm glad she's not dead. I would miss her dreadfully if she were.

We've got a few minutes to spare when we pull into the parking lot beside this tall church with huge windows. The windows are a pattern of stained-glass squares. It looks sort of modern. The parking lot is full except for several parking spaces marked for visitors.

"I guess that's us," Randy says as he pulls into one of the visitor spaces.

"Guess so."

Randy steps out of the Jeep and comes around to my door. I watch him as he comes and I have to say he looks very good in a suit. He's not wearing a tie, but he's got a white shirt on and a charcoal-gray sports jacket.

"Nice suit," I say as he opens my door.

"I didn't know what to wear."

I take his hand and step out of the Jeep. "I didn't know, either."

I'm standing right in front of him now and he's smiling at me.

"You look lovely," Randy says and he just keeps smiling into my eyes.

"Oh." I can't remember ever having a guy tell me I looked good when he was just looking at my eyes.

Of course, we can't kiss in the visitor's space of the church parking lot, but he does hold my hand as we walk across the parking lot and it's almost just as nice.

A raindrop falls on my head right about the time we get to the steps of the church. The sky is getting even grayer. Randy and I stop and hesitate at the top of the stairs. The church has heavy wooden double doors leading inside and they are closed. It's starting to rain in earnest now so I can understand why they would have the doors closed.

"I was hoping to be able to peek inside first," I say to Randy.

He's got a grim, determined look on his face. "I know. That way we could leave if we didn't like what we saw."

"I don't suppose there'll be anything too bad inside," I say. I never expected to face a commitment before I knew anything about the church. I wonder briefly if all of those stained-glass window panes are to keep the people outside from looking in or the people inside from looking out. Either way it's not good.

Randy tightens his hold on my hand and takes a step forward. "Well, here we go."

I have this strange sense that I'm crossing over some barrier as I step forward. Maybe this is how Alice felt when she slid down the rabbit hole and found herself in that strange, new wonderland of hers.

Chapter Ten

"Things do not change; we change."

—Henry David Thoreau

I brought this quote to a Sisterhood meeting one summer. I had pulled it out of an old book of my father's. I even brought the book with me to the meeting with a slip of paper marking the page that had the quote. My dad had underlined the words at some point. I thought of all of the times he had tried to change his drinking behavior and failed.

I remember Becca didn't like this quote. She thought we should be able to change things, not just ourselves. None of the rest of us felt we had lived long enough to have an opinion; we had never tried to make big changes. I never told the Sisterhood that the book belonged to my father or that he lived most of his life refusing to change.

* * *

The church is decorated for Christmas. Not with the gold garlands that my aunt uses in her house, but with real pine boughs and velvet burgundy ribbons. Because of the pine, everything smells like the outdoors. If I went by scent, I would say I was in a damp morning forest because the air also smells a little from the rain that is now falling steady.

There are rows and rows of oak pews on each side of a center aisle; the pews face a raised platform in the front. There's a pulpit on the platform and some rows of benches behind it that must be for the choir. Gleaming brass organ pipes line one side of the platform and the sound of organ music is soft in the background.

It's a very comfortable place.

There have to be a couple of hundred people in the church. Some of them are sitting in the pews and some of them are standing in the aisle talking with each other. There is lots of chatter and it seems like happy chatter. I always thought churches were more silent and somber and I'm glad to be proved wrong in this at least.

I see Marilee about the same time as she sees Randy and me. She gives us a little wave and starts walking toward us. I note with some satisfaction that she is wearing a dress much like mine.

I let go of Randy's hand and give Marilee a hug.

"You really came," Marilee says when we part. She is beaming.

"I said I would." Just because I didn't tell everyone all of my business years ago, it doesn't mean I lie. If I say I'll do something, I do it.

If Marilee hears the edge to my voice, she doesn't pay any attention to it. She motions for Randy and me to follow her. "Quinn is saving seats for us."

We barely get settled on the pew before the whole thing begins. We stand and sing a song. I'm pleased that I know the words. I didn't think I would know any of the songs, but I hadn't thought about it being Christmas. They are singing Christmas carols.

Some of the songs tell about Mary and her new baby so I think right away of the play. After today, there are only three more full days until Thursday when we have an afternoon dress rehearsal and then our opening-night performance. I'm looking forward to seeing everyone in costume.

There's a final song about the bright star that led the wise men to Jesus and then the pastor of the church gets up to the front and starts to talk. I had been hoping he would talk about Mary and I am not disappointed.

I had never thought about Mary's relationship to God before she was chosen. I know after she was chosen she had to know He was up to something in her life. But I had never thought about how she would have felt about God had He not chosen her at all. The pastor said he thought Mary would have accepted God's will even if He had decided she would be barren instead of being the mother of Jesus. Mary was not negotiating with God for a better position in the world; she only wanted to do what He wanted.

Of course, I already knew Mary wouldn't do well in my world. For the first time, though, I am beginning to wonder if I would have been able to cope in her world. As much as I chaff at my mother's insistence that I be treated like a princess, I have to say I can handle being treated as a princess much better than I could deal with being passed over altogether. Being barren for a woman in Mary's world would mean being almost invisible and without power. It could be cause for a divorce, for ridicule, for pity.

This is when I think back to the quote by Thoreau about change. I would have to change the inside of me to be like Mary and I don't know how to do that. I can change the outside of me a hundred different ways. But the inside? That seems beyond me.

The church service ends with a prayer.

Pastor Engstrom walks out and stands on the steps when church is over. People come up and greet Marilee and Quinn and then turn to meet Randy and me. The names of all of the people come and go fast, but the smiles are all sincere.

People line up to shake hands with Pastor Engstrom.

"Thanks for talking about Mary," I say when I reach the pastor.

He shakes my hand. "She's one of my favorite people in the Bible."

"Mine, too," I say.

"Carly's an understudy in a play about Mary," Marilee says from behind me. "She's been reading everything she can about her."

"Well, if I can answer any questions, let me know," the pastor says. "Marilee knows I have a question and answer group every Wednesday morning. You're more than welcome to come."

"Thanks. I might do that."

"It's at nine o'clock, the room's right through the side door on your left."

I nod and leave the church. Randy is beside me.

"Well, that was painless," Randy says as we walk toward his Jeep. "I was expecting some pressure to join up or something."

"I liked it."

Randy nods. "Me, too."

He sounds surprised and I can fully understand.

"It's not like the church I went to when I was a kid," he says as he opens the passenger side door. "I never did feel welcome in that church, but my mother insisted we go."

"You must have been young then, if it was while your mother was still alive." I climb up into the passenger seat.

Randy nods and closes the door.

I wait for him to walk around to the driver's door. I'm starting to get a new picture of Randy.

"Why weren't you welcome in the church?" I ask when he's settled.

He looks over at me as he starts the ignition. "We were poor, even for Fontana. And there were lots of us kids. I think people just saw us as an untidy jumble."

His childhood had been very different than mine. He'd grown up as a weed and I'd been pruned to within an inch of my life. I could see though why a woman with the San Marino look would appeal to him now. I suppose we all need to make our peace with our childhood in some way.

Randy suggested we go to brunch at the Ritz-Carlton and he was so proud when he offered that I told him it would be my pleasure.

The Ritz-Carlton brunch was elegant as usual. Because it was so close to Christmas, they had garlands of pine looping along the wide staircase that led to the downstairs dining room and the outdoor terrace where the brunch was served. A woman was playing carols on a harp in a corner and an ice sculpture of a reindeer stood on the round table that had the sushi bar.

I figured my mother told Randy to take me here. It is a beautiful place, though, and they have these little desserts that are so puffy and filled with such smooth crèmes that they could have come from a real French bakery.

By the time he takes me home, I'm exhausted. I like Randy. He's easy to be with. My fatigue isn't about him; it's all me.

* * *

I couldn't wait to write in the journal and, now that I am, I'm just letting it all out.

I don't know what's wrong with me. It's like it's getting harder and harder to pretend to be the person people see when they look at me. I've been trying to convince myself that the outside shell doesn't matter, but I'm beginning to think I'm all wrong. The outside shell *does* matter when it doesn't match who you are inside.

I blame it on Mary. Not the actress who's playing Mary, but the real one who lived thousands of years ago.

She was quiet, but I can tell from the reading I've done that she was who she was. She wasn't a dressed-up doll pretending to be a princess. She didn't expect special treatment or try to be a blonde when she was a brunette. I know they didn't have designer brands back then, but I don't think she would have looked at them anyway.

Mary had better things to do than to try and become a star. She had a baby to raise and a God to please.

After I've written everything out in the journal, I sit for a while on the balcony and think about Mary and that Thoreau quote. I need to make some changes in my life and I'm wondering how I can do it.

I have the journal still on my lap and I think about adding an addendum to what I have said because I don't want anyone to feel bad if they care about designer labels. That life may be the right one for some people; it's just that it doesn't fit me anymore.

I miss myself. The person I used to be before I was the Rose Queen and then got cancer was different than the person I am today. I think my mother and I got so caught up in the Rose Queen business that we took everything too far.

We changed my hair. We changed my walk. We changed my wardrobe.

And then, when I had cancer, none of it mattered to me so it was easier just to keep the Rose Queen fantasy going in my mother's mind than to revert back to being me. I realize now I should have made some changes anyway.

My mother has grown accustomed to the new me. I don't know how she will react if I change myself now. I love my mother. I know she drives me nuts. But I want her to be happy with me.

Once Christmas is over, though, I'm going to dye my hair back to my normal color. I might get a few clothes that aren't designer labels, too. I'll need them to do what I'm thinking I might do.

When Uncle Lou gets back from Italy, I'm going to ask him for a job waitressing at The Pews. I should have done it sooner. They always hire college students and I know one of the waitresses is going to quit in January. I can rent a small apartment or even a room somewhere in Pasadena and continue on with my classes until I get my degree. I've been taking lots of literature classes, but next semester I think I'll change to an education major and work on becoming an English teacher.

I know it might not seem like a lot, but if I am able to make all of these changes, I might feel back on the right track to being me.

Lizabett will be disappointed that I don't want to be a movie star and my mother will be disappointed that I'm not her blond creation. Randy will be—

Ah, I stop for a moment. I don't want to disappoint Randy. Now that I know more about his background, I really wonder if he'll like me when I've given up the San Marino look. It might be important to Randy to impress his friends with a girlfriend who looks like she's not just from the right side of the tracks but from the top of the hill as well.

Not that I plan to be ugly. Or plain.

Oh, dear, the more I think about this the more I think I better sleep on it before I make any firm decisions. One thing I am doing, though, is I am going to leave these pages in the journal right open. If anyone in the Sisterhood wants to see what I'm thinking, they are welcome to go right ahead and look.

And, if Becca ever reads it, I want to say I'm not holding anything back. There are no secrets here. I've learned my lesson. Please, forgive me.

I sit for a while longer on the balcony. A few days ago I strung some red and green Christmas lights around the railing here. No one can see this balcony from the street, so I don't clash with my aunt's gold and white Christmas fantasy out front. I guess I've always been more traditional than stylish when it comes right down to it. No one who's stylish does multicolor lights anymore. It's old-fashioned.

I have a few presents, wrapped and tucked away in my bedroom. I bought my mother a handblown glass Christmas ornament from Germany. She doesn't have this one in her collection and I know she'll be happy with it. I bought books for everyone else. Lizabett's present is a biography of Lucille Ball. I got a devotional book for Marilee that she had mentioned some time ago and I have a new mystery novel for Becca from her favorite author.

My mother and I always get my aunt a gift certificate to a spa and give my uncle a gift certificate for the golf course he uses. This year I've also knitted them both scarves.

I've knitted my dad a sweater and my mother mailed it to him a week or so ago.

I'm going to miss my dad at Christmas this year. I keep expecting him to be able to come home. I know his addiction is severe, but he can't stay in that treatment center forever. We need him back with us.

There's a knock on the doors leading out to this balcony and I turn to see my mother coming out with a couple of cups on a tray.

"Cocoa?" she asks.

"Thanks, Mom."

I take one cup of cocoa and motion to the other chair on the balcony. My mother sits down with her own cocoa and we watch the sunset together.

Chapter Eleven

"A book holds a house of gold."

—Chinese proverb

Rose brought this quote to us. She was determined that we all learn to enjoy reading. I think she had this vision of us reading through our chemo treatments. It didn't work like that, but we appreciated the thought anyway. Rose was always trying to think of things that would take our minds off of what we were going through even though she realized nothing could.

I don't have classes this week, so I head down to The Pews around ten o'clock on Monday morning. I want to be there in plenty of time for the lunch crowd so I can help. There's always more people coming into the diner during the week of Christmas and, since I'm hoping Randy will have some time to practice my lines with me, I should help out. It's only fair.

Even though I'm very comfortable now with the fact that I won't be onstage as Mary, I still want to learn the lines perfectly, just for myself. I have a feeling that's what Mary would do if she were in my place. Something can be good to do even if no one else ever sees it to applaud the fact. That's a very different concept than I've learned so far in my life. I no longer want to do things just because someone notices and applauds. I'm not sure how well I can manage with this new approach to life, but I want to try.

I wrap a dish towel around my waist shortly after I arrive at The Pews. One of the waitresses has called in sick and Randy is getting everything ready for the lunch crowd. It's a good thing I came down and I like feeling needed. I'm going to stand at the steel counter in the kitchen and slice tomatoes.

First, though, I need to get ready. I don't have a hairnet so I wrap a bandana around my head like a turban. We're very conscious of health codes at The Pews and everyone always has their hair covered when they're near the food.

"Ah," Randy says when he turns and sees me with my hair covered. "I guess it's necessary, but it's a pity. I love your hair."

"Oh." I pause and then step over to the sink to wash my hands. "You know blond isn't my natural color, don't you?"

"Well, whatever you do to your hair, you look great."

"I'm thinking of changing it," I say as I scrub my

hands, but Randy is already back over at the grill flipping the chicken breasts he's cooking for the Chinese chicken salad.

"Sounds good," he says.

Just then I hear the bell on the outside door ring and I know a customer has arrived. I look out into the dining room and I see that six people have just seated themselves at a table. I dry my hands and go out to get their orders.

That starts the lunch rush.

A couple of hours later, the hungry hordes are gone and Randy and I have a chance to go into the Sisterhood room so that I can practice my lines. We've gone over my lines together enough that we only need the script here and there as a reminder.

It's fun to practice with Randy. The script is a little offbeat and he gives himself to the role of Joseph with grand flourishes and enthusiasm.

"I had a dream," he says dramatically.

We're sitting on the edge of the table, waiting for the place in the script where we'll be pretending the table is the back of the pickup truck. Randy sets a couple of plastic pitchers around us to represent the chickens that will also be riding in the back of the old pickup.

The Depression-era play does pick up a lot of the flavor of the times.

We pick up the script from the beginning and run through the main scenes several times before we're interrupted.

I hear a knock on the French doors and I look up to see Lizabett.

"Hey," I say as I slide off the table.

Lizabett comes into the room. "I thought you'd be here practicing."

Ordinarily, Lizabett and I would both be here about this time, but since we're out of school for Christmas break and not keeping to our usual schedule, I'm surprised to see her.

"I was doing some last-minute shopping," Lizabett says as she holds up a red bag she's carrying. "I have everybody's gift except the ones for my brothers. I never know what to get them."

"Socks," Randy says. "Guys always need more socks."

Lizabett wrinkles up her nose. "That's not very exciting."

Randy shrugs. "It's either socks or expensive electronics. Or maybe season tickets to the Lakers. Or sporting equipment. Do any of them golf?"

"No," Lizabett says and then grins. "But they used to love to play horse basketball with the hoop at my mother's house. There aren't any balls left there anymore, but if my brothers had one, they'd love to play. They're so competitive."

"Still?" Randy asks slowly. "I mean now that Quinn's—well, is he allowed to be competitive since he's become a Christian?"

"Oh." Lizabett stops and thinks. "I don't know." Lizabett looks at me.

I shrug. "I wonder, too. All I can say is that Mary wouldn't take any pleasure in beating her brothers at basketball."

Randy is frowning by now. "That kind of takes all of the joy out of life."

The three of us stand there for a minute or two thinking about the ramifications of being a Christian.

"Quinn still watches television," Lizabett finally offers. "I think it must be okay to do things. He's not like a monk or anything."

"I'll have to ask him," Randy says. "I've been thinking about what it'd be like since I went to church yesterday. I just can't picture giving up sports."

"Not all sports are competitive, are they?" I ask.

"If they're not competitive, they're just exercise like walking around the block," Randy says firmly. "I like to keep score. It pushes me to do better. I like playing against my friends that have turned pro even though I lose."

I hadn't realized Randy was seriously thinking about our visit to church just like I had been.

"It might say something in those books we borrowed from Quinn," I say as I point to the bookshelf behind us.

There are a dozen books on that shelf now. Lizabett has brought them here one book at a time over the past couple of weeks.

"If we don't find something there, I'm planning to go to Pastor Engstrom's group on Wednesday morning. I could ask him," I offer.

Randy nods. "If I can't figure it out, maybe I'll go with you."

"Good."

Lizabett looks at us. "If everybody is going, let me know. I don't want to be left out."

"You won't be," I assure her with a smile.

When Marilee comes out of her office to join us, no one says anything about our questions. I notice we're all looking at her though to see if she seems to be doing anything different than she used to do.

I clean off some of the tables in the diner and Lizabett refills some of the condiment holders. We serve the dinner crowd and wait for it to grow quiet again.

"Still watching those baseball games?" I finally ask Marilee when we are leaning on the counter in the main part of the diner.

The Pews will be closing in half an hour. Lizabett is also at the counter and Randy is restocking the glasses in the rack over the counter.

I notice Randy stops working with the glasses when I ask my question.

"Well, not now," Marilee says.

"I knew it," Lizabett says with a snap of her fingers. "Too competitive."

"No, that's not it," Marilee says slowly as she looks at Lizabett a little strangely. "It's just not baseball season right now."

"Oh," Lizabett says.

Marilee looks at me. "What's this about baseball all of a sudden?"

I can't think of anything to say before Marilee answers her own question. "Sorry I asked—it's Christmas. No one should ask questions like that at Christmas."

"Oh, yeah," Lizabett agrees.

"So." Randy leans against the counter. "You don't have a problem with competition now that you're a Christian?"

"Oh, no," Marilee says. She sounds a little startled. "I mean if it's a fair competition and all. Why?"

"I just wanted to be sure," Randy says as he turns back to the glasses.

"I would have a problem with making fun of someone who lost," Marilee adds. "And being compulsive about a sport—you know, to where you didn't think of anything else ever and neglected your kids or your friends or your *life*."

"Well, of course," Randy agrees. "That's only common sense."

"What's all this about competition? You're not planning to try to get on that new reality show, are you?" Marilee looks at Randy with a frown. "Because I'm not sure that they play fair at all. Carly was telling me about it and—"

Randy holds up his hands. "I don't even know anything about a reality show."

Now, everyone's looking at me.

"All I know is what I told Marilee," I say to Randy.

"There's supposed to be a producer coming to one of the performances for the play to look people over to be in this new reality show they're going to film in Cancún."

"You're not hoping to be on that, are you?" Randy asks, looking at me. "Those new shows are ruthless. I'd rather play football with the Mafia."

In the play, Joseph makes a reference to the Mafia. They're the ones out to get the three wise men instead of King Herod so they're on our minds.

"Don't worry," I say. "I'm not going to be on the stage so the producer won't even see me. Besides, I think I could handle a reality show."

All three of my friends just look at me. Marilee, Lizabett and Randy. None of them look like they agree.

"Really," I add. "I'm tougher than I look."

"You're a cream puff," Lizabett says.

"Not that you're not tough inside," Marilee adds loyally. "And that's where it counts."

I wonder if they'd say something like that if I'd gotten my black belt in karate instead of that crown in the beauty pageant.

"At least, I'd get a trip to Cancún," I persist just to show them I'm made of stern stuff and am not afraid of what a reality show could do to me.

"If you want to go to Cancún, I'll take you," Randy says.

Well, that takes the attention off of me. Marilee and Lizabett stop to stare at Randy.

"Really?" Lizabett says. "Cancún is halfway around the world."

"And expensive," Marilee adds.

Randy shrugs. "Carly's worth it."

"Well, of course, she's *worth* it," Marilee agrees. "But—"

"No one's really thinking about going to Cancún," I say. "It's just a for instance. Like a maybe if—"

People start talking about places they'd like to vacation and we get talking about European river cruises and African safaris. It all makes the Cancún trip sound pretty tame. I would imagine that the reality show has something else in mind besides a beach vacation in the sun, but that's what I think of when I think of Cancún.

Randy is locking the back doors to the diner when it occurs to me.

"Nobody would think Becca couldn't do a reality show," I say.

Lizabett nods. "She'd tear the heart out of her competition."

"Well, she'd at least hold her own," Marilee adds.

"I miss her," I say and we all nod.

"Her e-mail said she'll be back in touch soon," Marilee says.

"She better be," I say. Becca might be able to tear the heart out of her competition, but I'll stand firm with her if I have to. I'm not willing to lose her friendship.

Randy drives me home and I find I like riding along in his Jeep in the dark. The Jeep rides rougher than my parents' car, but there's a sense of adventure from riding up a little higher. Besides, Randy is here.

"Are you really thinking about this Christian stuff?" I ask.

He nods in the dark. "Trying to figure it out. That Joseph was some guy, you know."

"Yeah," I say. It makes me feel good that Randy is learning from Joseph and I am learning from Mary. Even if we're not really in the play, I feel like we have the parts down.

It's not late when we get to my house, so Randy parks on the street and we walk up the drive to my uncle's house.

"Want to come in and say hello to my mother?" I ask as we get to the back steps. "It'll make her day."

"Sure," Randy says.

He doesn't stay long, but he gives my mother enough to talk about for days. I know it's going to be coming. All the talk about how handsome he is and how polite and how everything that is wonderful. Surprisingly enough, though, it doesn't matter. If it makes my mother happy, I'm glad. My mother has been looking a little depressed lately and I'm worried about her.

I walk Randy back down the stairs and we share a goodbye kiss just outside the door.

"Thanks for helping me with my lines," I say after a kiss or two.

Um, make that three kisses.

Randy smiles. "And thanks for sharing your mother with me."

I grin. "My pleasure."

I don't even need a kiss to make that one sweet.

After Randy leaves, I take the journal out onto the balcony and sit for a while writing about the events of the day. I realize that I forgot to ask Randy some probing questions to figure out what to get him for Christmas. I don't know for sure if he's getting me a present, but I think he might and I want to be ready. I was thinking about giving him the scarf I'm knitting, but it's not a scarf I started with him in mind. If I do give him something, I want it to be more personal.

Randy had mentioned that guys like socks, but I hope I can do better than that since he sort of offered me a trip to Cancún. I mean, I know we're not going, but still I think he was half-sincere. An offer like that deserves at least a tie.

There are only two more days until Thursday. That's the day when we have the the opening performance for the play and the party afterwards at my uncle's house.

That reminds me. I definitely need to find a time to talk with my aunt tomorrow and find out what she needs me to do for the party.

I close the journal and sit for a few minutes in

the quiet dark of the night. Since no one's watching, I look up and give God a little wave good-night. A slight breeze blows by me suddenly and I wonder if He's waving back at me. I kind of hope He is. Wouldn't that be something?

Chapter Twelve

"The most successful people are those who are good at plan B."

—James Yorke

I brought this quote to the Sisterhood and it still amuses me. I am not a plan B kind of a person. None of us in the Sisterhood are. I wondered when we first talked about this quote if having cancer made us less flexible than we would have been otherwise. It seemed like so much was out of our control that we hung on for dear life to those few things we thought we could control.

I didn't know I would need a plan B the first thing on Tuesday morning, but I did. I stopped to talk to my aunt before I left for my play rehearsal. We are standing in the doorway of the front door.

"I've heard Max Sullivan is going to be here," my

aunt says. She is rubbing her hands in anticipation or worry, I don't know which. "I hear he's the power behind all of those new movies. I can't wait to meet him. Do you think he might come speak to our garden club some time?"

My aunt belongs to the San Marino Garden Club, the club that had part of its winter home tour at my uncle's house last weekend. She would be ecstatic to bring in a well-known speaker from the movie industry. The other women would be all over something like that.

"I don't know," I say, wishing I could do better to please her. My aunt is always easier to live around when she has her way. "I don't know him at all."

"Well, he's going to be watching your play before he comes to the party," my aunt says. "Surely, he'll want to meet the actors. You can ask him then."

"I'm an understudy," I say. "I doubt I'll be there if he does meet the actors."

"An understudy?" my aunt says with a frown.

My aunt has a fine smooth face; her salon appointments see to that. Frowning is her only vice. She wears sunblock; she eats the right vitamins; she has her skin renewed regularly with some kind of a facial. I guess she can't stop the frowning though.

"It's okay," I say. "Really. I'm fine with being an understudy for Mary."

"Maybe if your uncle spoke to the director."

"No, no. That's not necessary. The parts are already assigned. I'm fine with being an understudy."

If the girl with the butterfly tattoo only knew how close she is to losing her part, she'd be screeching at me about now. I have no doubt that my uncle could throw enough weight around to intimidate the director of the play, especially when the director is having the cast party at my uncle's house.

"It wouldn't be fair to change things now," I say.

"I just don't like to see you overlooked."

I have never seen my aunt being this nice to me. "Is everything okay?"

"Well, yes," my aunt says hesitantly. "I think so."

There's no early sun this morning and the house looks shadowed inside.

"It's my mother, isn't it?"

I never understand why people don't tell the families when someone is sick. I've always known that, if something was wrong with my mother, I would be the very last one to know. And she has been looking so frail lately. Like she's sad and expecting worse to come.

"No, no." My aunt looks startled. "It's the food."

"Food? For the party?" I ask in relief.

My aunt nods. "Our regular caterer is already booked and it's only two days notice for the party so I don't think we can get anyone else that's any good. So, I was wondering if that place you go—you know, the place—if they would do it?"

"The Pews?"

My aunt nods. "We'll pay, of course."

"I can ask."

The Pews doesn't ordinarily do catering, but when I get there and mention it to Marilee, she thinks it would be a great idea. She sees that there will be enough of the right kind of people at the party to jump-start a side catering business for The Pews.

"Who knows? We might even start doing this sort of thing. For right now we have the kitchen space to fix the food and Randy has a Jeep so we can haul big pans of things for the party. What kind of food does your aunt want?"

Marilee and I are sitting in our Sisterhood room at The Pews. We're waiting for the coffee in our cups to cool a little.

"Little bites of things. Something that will impress people."

"That means silver trays," Marilee says. "And we'll need to hire some waitstaff."

"I could pass around a tray."

I think of the black shirt and white blouse I was going to wear to church last Sunday.

Marilee nods. "We might all need to help, but I think it would be fun."

"We'd be doing something together," I agree.

"You'll need to talk to Randy about the menu," Marilee tells me. "I'll go check on our stock of plastic glasses. No, wait." She looks at me. "I suppose we should use the real ones?"

I nod. "If you want it to look elegant."

Marilee reaches behind her and pulls a white tablet off the bookshelf. "I'll need to make a list."

I swear, Marilee could launch a war if she had enough lists. She's one of the most organized people I know. I've wondered for a while now if she isn't a little bored with her job at The Pews. I know her heart is here. But, like I said, she could run any kind of a campaign. She's just not using all of her talents at her job here.

Marilee is still making lists when Lizabett comes to The Pews and asks me if I want company for my rehearsal today. I nod. Lizabett enjoys watching the play take shape and its fun to sit with her and see everyone run through their lines.

Of course, Lizabett keeps hoping the director will yell, "Cut!" and call for the understudy for Mary to step forward, but I'm happy enough watching the butterfly lady do the honors.

If Randy weren't needed at the grill, I would like him to see the role of Joseph played in rehearsal. Joseph is a short, stocky guy who looks like a computer technician. When he looks at Mary, though, he looks at her with clear fondness on his face. The director was smart to get a boyfriend-girlfriend combo to play Joseph and Mary. It makes for some believable acting.

By the time Lizabett and I slip into the church where everyone is rehearsing, the play is almost ready to go on. Since I'm technically part of the cast, Lizabett and I get to sit in the first few rows of the church so we can see everything well.

The stage is almost finished being built at the

front of the church. Someone has painted some fantastic backgrounds of dusty landscapes with farmhouses in the distance and what looks like dead grass on the ground.

Now that I've read the New Testament a few times, I can see how the dryness in the first part of the play is symbolic. It is what the world was like before Jesus was born. All of those dusty images could make a person thirsty. No wonder Mary goes on about tomatoes when she gets closer to their destination.

"They want to make you long for Christmas," I whisper to Lizabett. "All that dust in the beginning and then the gradual greening as the big night arrives."

Lizabett is looking at the side of the stage where some of the other props are stacked.

"Is that Motel 6 sign supposed to be for the inn?" she asks.

I nod. "And the manger is a gas station."

"I can't imagine Jesus being born in a gas station," Lizabett says.

"Actually, he's born in the restroom of the gas station. The station is closed for the night."

"Wow."

"Mary and Joseph were poor," I say.

Joseph's understudy comes down the aisle and sits in front of us. He turns around and nods. He and I don't actually know each other, but we nod at each other just to show that we both know it could be the two of us up there on the stage if disaster suddenly struck.

It kind of bothers me that Joseph's understudy looks a lot more like the actor playing Joseph than I look like the butterfly woman playing Mary. It just makes it so plain to me that the director chose me as the understudy because he wanted to use my uncle's house and the understudy role was the least he could give me. And I mean the absolute least.

I know this is the way Hollywood works even on small productions like this one. It's all about who you know or, more accurately, who the people you are meeting know and whether they are willing to introduce you to them later.

I brought the journal with us this afternoon. Not because I think either Lizabett or I will do much writing. But because it feels good to have it with us. I never thought I'd feel this way about the journal. But it's a part of me like my cell phone and my bus pass.

I wonder if it's because I am starting to like being responsible for the journal. It's like carrying the heart of the Sisterhood around.

"They missed that one," the Joseph understudy turns around and whispers at me. "If they can't learn the lines, they shouldn't be up there."

"They're probably just nervous," I whisper back.

He grunts in disgust. "I could do better."

I just shrug at him. I might have said the same kind of a thing a week or so ago. Its easy to put people down instead of lifting them up. "The important thing is the play."

Well, that made the understudy turn back around and face the stage.

"Did I sound stuffy?" I turn to Lizabett and whisper softly. "I didn't mean to. It's just that—"

Lizabett nods. "You're right to take it seriously. It's Mary's story. Well, and Joseph's, too—and the baby's at the end."

The lights are starting to dim as the old pickup truck onstage bounces along to the motel that is flashing a No Vacancy sign. This is one of my favorite parts, because I see how worried Joseph is about Mary. Not that I wouldn't be worried, too, since a baby is going to be born any minute now and he's the one who has to make the arrangements and there's no 911 to call.

Joseph talks with the man inside the motel and the desk clerk keeps shaking his head. Finally, the desk clerk reaches under the counter and brings up a short stack of neatly folded towels.

"Here. It's the best I can do," he says to Joseph. "And the restroom is always open at the station across the street. At least it has heat and it has a big hallway in front."

"Thanks." Joseph takes the towels and goes back to the pickup truck.

I sit here and think about Christmas. I've always thought how terrible the innkeeper was to not go upstairs and kick some of his guests out of their room so there'd be a place for Jesus to be born. But I see we treat lots of people as though they're not as important as we think we are. I guess I shouldn't say we. The truth is I haven't even passed out towels to people in need very often.

It's easy to enjoy the Christmas nativity scene when it's a few plastic figures nestled into a manger. It all looks kind of cozy. And anyone who has pets knows a few animals around only adds to the charm. But when I think about the manger as being a cement-floored restroom at the back of a gas station with only a few towels for comfort, I start to realize that Mary must have been scared.

She had to trust God a lot. Or she would have unraveled completely. Not only was she having a baby, she was part of the greatest miracle of all time. I still haven't quite wrapped my mind around that virgin birth part.

I have the Sisterhood journal sitting in my lap and I grab it a little tighter.

I'm almost surprised when the shepherds show up. They are farm laborers and they have a wire cage filled with chickens. I know the director used chickens for animals instead of sheep because they're smaller and fit on the stage better, but I think he might be on to something. Chickens are humble creatures and I like that.

I see the farm laborers all taking off their caps as they look at the baby.

Lizabett sighs when the play is over. For the first time since she's started watching the play, she doesn't comment that I should be in the lead Mary role. I know that means she's looked past her ambitions for me and is seeing the story.

"The baby would have been cold if the desk clerk hadn't given them those towels," Lizabett finally said.

I nod.

Lizabett makes a stop once we get to Pasadena. She pulls right up into the parking lot on Lake and Walnut and puts five dollars in the red bucket that the Salvation Army person has there. I put in another five dollars.

"God bless you," the Salvation Army man says.

"Thank you," we answer right back.

We drive on to one of the parking lots just off of Colorado. Lizabett parks her car there and we walk over to The Pews. The stores on Colorado are all decorated for Christmas with red swags from the streetlights and lots of twinkle lights in the windows.

I picked up my complimentary play tickets before I left the rehearsal and I will give Marilee and Randy their tickets. I already gave Lizabett her ticket. I will have to leave Becca's ticket at The Pews.

"You know, the best thing we did in a long time was to find a place for Joy to stay," I say to Lizabett as I open the door to The Pews.

"Randy's the one who did that," Lizabett says as she steps over the threshold.

"Well, and Becca brought her to our attention," I say as I follow her into the diner.

Now that I think about it, my contribution was more audience participation than anything. It's not an easy thing to realize you might not like to be treated like a princess anymore, but that it's still the way you know how to live.

I'm a little subdued as I give Marilee her ticket to the play.

"Can I do anything to help?" I ask Marilee as we stand by the main counter inside the diner.

"Mushrooms," she says as she leads me to the kitchen. "We're making crab-stuffed mushrooms for the party tomorrow and we have lots of de-capping to do."

The kitchen counters are full of boxes and trays.

"Hi," Randy says to me with a quick smile. He's standing at the grill putting a sauce on some tiger shrimp. "Welcome to toothpick town."

Randy reaches over to a nearby tray and gets one of the strawberries on a toothpick. He holds it out to me. "Sweets for the sweet."

Marilee groans.

Randy chuckles. "Hey, I'm grilling here. I don't have time to think of new poetry."

"It's lovely," I say as I walk over and take the strawberry. "My favorite."

I start working. I think it's a nice touch that someone has thought to include baby tomatoes stuffed with cream cheese and chives.

"You?" I ask Randy as I point at the tomatoes.

Randy nods. "I did it for Mary."

I can't help but think that that's just the kind of thing Joseph would do. I hope so. I've never heard much said about romance in the nativity story, but I hope that Mary looked at Joseph and felt her heart pound a little faster.

I doubt he was handsome, of course. There's no indication of that. I glance up at Randy. I think he's the kind of guy that starts out looking real handsome, but as you get to know him better and better you don't think of him as being handsome so much because there are so many other things that crowd into your mind when you think about him.

Randy is a good man.

I think about that as I'm lying in my bed later that night and it's not a dreamy sort of thing. I care about Randy. I want him to have everything in life he's ever wanted. The problem is that I think what he might want is a San Marino kind of a girlfriend.

I could be that. I have been that. All I need to do is to stop any changing I'm inclined to do. The thought of it doesn't make me happy. I lie there for a while and then I finally go to sleep.

Chapter Thirteen

"We know what we are, but know not what we may be."

—William Shakespeare

Lizabett wrote this quote out on index cards for each of us one evening. She wanted us to tack it to our bulletin boards. This was when her hair was beginning to grow back and she was blossoming. Her mind was filled with possibilities. We were not as positive as she was about the future, but we were all happy that she was flitting around us like she was. It was good to see her happy.

I wake up and feel excited. Even before I open my eyes I know this is going to be a special day. This is the day of the opening performance of the play and then the party afterward. The play will go on smoothly without me, but I have a feeling I'm going to be needed for the party. Who else is going to finish stuffing the mushrooms? Or make sure that we find those fancy cocktail napkins and the toothpicks with the silver ribbons on the end? And the music? I wonder if anyone has thought of background music; I'll need to check.

I put that old flannel robe on and go sit for a few minutes on the balcony with a cup of coffee in my hands. It's extra cold this morning. I can't see the sun rise from this side of the house, but I watch the leaves in the trees start to take shape as the sun gradually rises on the other side. The morning always smells damp and earthy because of all of the plants and shrubs around my uncle's house. I never appreciate the leaves as much as I do just before Christmas; I know most places only have barren trees at that time of year, but here we have a bountiful mix of leaves and bare branches. It's beautiful.

I sip some of my coffee and search the sky as it lightens. This looking at the sky thing has become a habit when I sit on the balcony these days. Not that I expect to see a sign from God written across the heavens exactly. I just wonder if He's looking at me.

There were many times in my life when I would have hid if I thought God was looking my way, but I don't feel that way anymore. I drink the rest of my coffee slowly. I feel almost companionable sitting here letting God look at me if He wants. Learning about Mary has done this for me.

I see a light go on in the hallway so I know my

mother is up. I go back inside. Today's a big day. I better get started. I'll take the bus to The Pews and get to work.

I put the Sisterhood journal in my bag and kiss my mom goodbye. I wonder if I should be carrying the journal around so much. Maybe if I left it at The Pews, Becca would sneak in when no one's there and write a note or something. At least then we'd know she was still a part of us. I've begun to wonder if the others blame me for making Becca mad.

There are more customers than usual at The Pews. It's because it's so close to Christmas. Everybody wants to go out and have a good time. And, of course, they think of The Pews first when they want to do that because it's the best place to meet friends.

I put my jacket and my bag in the Sisterhood room. I carefully take the journal out of my bag and set it on the shelf by the table so everyone can see it. Then I go to the kitchen.

There is a lot to do. Randy gives me a thumbs-up signal when I walk through the door. He's flipping pancakes on the grill for the breakfast crowd. He hasn't even had a chance to start on the stuff for the party. It's easy to see the small tomatoes need to be washed and cored so I get to it.

After an hour or so, Lizabett comes in to help as well. She's wearing a jacket. "Have you been outside lately? It's cold out there."

"Well, it's hot in here with all the cooking."

"Don't forget you have the dress rehearsal this

afternoon," Randy says to us. "Leave extra time in case it rains and the freeways are backed up."

Lizabett had already offered to drive me to the dress rehearsal and we plan to leave after lunch.

"I don't know." I look up from the radishes I'm cutting into the shape of roses. "Maybe I should call in. There's so much to do to get ready for tonight. And I'm not really needed at the dress rehearsal."

"You don't know that," Lizabett says. "Maybe Mary will break her leg or something."

Lizabett sounds a little too cheerful at the thought of someone's broken bones.

"She'll be there no matter what," I tell Lizabett. "She's not going to miss her chance to impress the producer for that reality show. Believe me. She'd do the play if the church was on fire."

"Still, we should be there just in case. You can't lose hope. People have panic attacks or fall into comas all the time."

"Comas! I wouldn't want that to happen."

Lizabett just grins up at me. "I'll be back."

Hi, this is Lizabett writing in the journal. I saw it on the shelf and I thought I should record this momentous event. I just know something's going to happen so Carly gets on that stage. We've come too far to stop short now. Of course, I hope no one dies or anything. And a coma? Well, maybe not. But a little nudge couldn't hurt. Maybe some temporary amnesia or a pressing need to see a psychiatrist.

I don't want to freak Carly out by telling her my thoughts, but I figure it's okay to write them down here. I've prayed she'll get onstage and I think it's going to happen.

I also saw what Carly wrote about Becca and I want to say that I don't blame anyone for Becca being mad. We all know Becca well enough to know that she has her own opinions. No one makes her feel any way she doesn't want to feel. I've been thinking about it, though, and I have to wonder why Becca is so upset. I don't think she would be that upset with me if I was hiding the fact that I'm really some kind of big-time heiress with a trust fund waiting for me. Which I'm not, of course. But if I was, Becca would be able to adapt.

I think Becca just always envied Carly a little bit and that's why she's so angry. I used to watch Becca when we were talking sometimes and I noticed she always looked to Carly to see what she thought first. Maybe if she had not cared so much to begin with it wouldn't hurt so much now.

Well, I've gotta go. Carly has her hands full helping with the food for this party tonight. I know we're all helping, but Carly is doing the work of ten people. She deserves that part in the play.

Bye from Lizabett.

"There's no need to thank me," Lizabett announces when she comes back into the kitchen. "I did it for you."

"What?"

"Started the record of your big day in the Sisterhood journal. Somebody needs to write it down."

I wince. "I hope you didn't pray for some catastrophe to stop the actress from playing Mary."

Lizabett stood still. "I prayed, but I didn't say there needed to be a catastrophe."

"Good." I wrap the last chestnut in bacon and set it on the cookie sheet with the others, ready to go into the oven at the last minute. I'd already frosted the grapes with a sugared meringue and stuck them on toothpicks to put them in the freezer. I'm going to use them to decorate the platters. We're going with an icy winter look.

Lizabett makes encouraging remarks all during the time that she's driving me to the church where the play will be performed.

I am glad we made the trip when I see Joseph's understudy huddled in his usual place in the second row. He looks like a refugee who was turned back at the border for being too pathetic to let in. He could use some comfort and cheer and he's the closest thing to a partner I have in this business. We understudy people need to stick together. Acting can be a cruel business.

"Maybe there'll be another role next time," I say softly to him as Lizabett and I slip into our usual seats behind him.

I hear a rumble of some sort from the understudy.

Lizabett leans forward and puts her hand on his shoulder. "Don't feel bad."

He turns around and glares at us. He opens his mouth like he's going to say something and nothing comes out but a croak. He swallows and tries again. "Can't talk."

His voice sounds like it's coming from a distant cavern. His eyes look like he has a fever and his nose is red.

"He's got laryngitis," Lizabett says as she looks at me. "He should be home in bed."

The understudy shakes his head.

"Big day," he manages to say.

"But it's not like they need us here," I say. "Surely, no one would mind if you were home taking care of yourself. They could call you if they needed you to come down here."

"I want the reality show," the understudy croaks before his voice gives out completely and he turns around to face the stage. His shoulders hunch up like he's getting ready to cough.

"Maybe we should move a little," Lizabett whispers. We move down a few feet. It's not like he and I are that close as partners.

"That reality show has everyone acting strange," I complain. "I bet the producers just start these rumors and then never even show up. They're just hoping that, if they torment enough people, someone will watch their show if only out of spite."

I still don't think it's right for all of the attention to be on this mysterious reality show instead of the astonishing real story our play is trying to tell people. If God wanted to, He could show these people a reality show or two.

The lights in the church are dimmed and it's time for the dress rehearsal to begin.

A man at the side of the stage plays a little jazz music on a saxophone and before long the curtain will slowly open. A soft spotlight is supposed to focus on Mary. She will be wearing a mud-colored dress and her hair will be bound up in some khaki scarf that's made of stiff cotton. I guess there wasn't any fabric softener back then, either. Anyway, she will be looking at the scorched ground of a wheat field. The stage set will show a run-down farmhouse in the distance with a forlorn gray sheet on the clothesline.

I know what will be there because I've seen the pieces of this play being put together. I look at my watch. The director is running late. He should have already raised the curtain.

By now there should be a flash of lightening and the angel should have appeared.

Instead, I see two arms part the curtains and the director comes out in front. He shields his eyes from the spotlight.

"Understudies!" he calls out. "Where are the understudies?"

Lizabett squeals and grabs my arm. "Here! She's here!"

The director looks down at the rows close to the stage and searches the faces as though he's trying to decide which ones belong to his understudies. I raise my hand. Joseph's understudy gives a wracking cough.

"Get up here," the director says.

"Yes!" Lizabett screams again.

I walk right up onstage and Joseph's understudy comes along with me. The guy doing the spotlight shines it on us and the other light is dimmed.

The Joseph understudy coughs as we stand on the stage in front of the curtain.

"What's wrong with you?" the director says to him.

"No voice," the understudy croaks out so weakly I can barely hear him.

"You can't talk?" the director says as he runs his hand over his hair and starts to pace in front of us. "What next? First the real actors get snowed in up at Big Bear and then the one producer calls and cancels for some half-brained reason which I don't even understand. Just because his kid had to go to the hospital. Can't his wife handle that? He probably had a bigger play to go see."

I wish the director would back up. "The other Mary got snowed in?"

"I—" the understudy starts to say something, but his voice dies altogether and only air comes out.

The director turns to me. "You'll have to feed him his lines."

"But—"

"Yeah, it could work. You say your lines and then you step to the side and say Joseph's lines as well."

The man on the saxophone hits a deep, melancholy note on his instrument as he shakes his head.

The director turns to the saxophone man. "I suppose you have a better idea?"

"I need to go home," the understudy manages to say. His dedication to the play obviously ended when he heard the producer dropped out.

The director looks around blankly. "Well, we have to at least have a body walking around. People could deal with an invisible angel, but we can't have an imaginary Joseph. A silent Joseph is better than that."

The understudy backs away.

The director watches the understudy walk off the stage. "Coward. Just because the play is going to bomb, that's no excuse for abandoning it no matter how sick you are."

"It's not going to bomb," I say. This is Mary's story. It's the greatest story ever told. "I know someone who can play Joseph. He knows all the lines."

The director looks at me like I've just announced the Messiah is going to be born on his stage, after all. Which I guess, in a way, is what I have announced.

"Really?" the director asks. "We've got three hundred tickets sold for tonight."

"I'll ask this guy if he'll do it."

"No, you'll *beg* him to do it. What am I saying? I'll beg him to do it. What's his number?"

The director whips out his cell phone and has Randy called before the rest of us can take a deep breath.

"Yes!" the director shouts as he snaps his cell phone shut. "We've got a show to put on!"

The cell phone rings just as he puts it back in his pocket and he answers it.

"For you?" he says as he hands the phone to me.

I think it's going to be Randy, but it's not. It's the butterfly woman who was supposed to play Mary.

"Is it true?" she asks me. "That the producer cancelled and isn't coming to the opening?"

"That's what I heard."

"Then I'm not going to bother trying to get a ride down the mountain. He's probably going to come to the second showing then."

"Probably," I agree.

There's a moment's silence. "I hope you didn't think you were going to be able to perform in all of the productions."

"I'm happy just to do the opening."

And I am.

I must admit there is something electrifying about getting ready for the opening. Everyone is scurrying around getting more costumes since the other Mary wore a different size than I do. Fortunately, there's no shortage of mud-colored dresses that look like tents.

"But your hair," the costume designer frets. "Mary can't be a blonde. We'll need to dig out a wig for you. The hair has to be brown. Black might be okay, but not blond."

"I don't need a wig," I say. "I've been meaning to go back to my natural color anyway. Brown."

The costume woman leaves the stage to go back in her room to find out what she has for me to wear. The director is off talking to the saxophone player. The shepherds are taking a coffee break.

Lizabett has moved up onstage next to me and she looks at me. "Are you sure? Dying your hair? This isn't just some spur-of-the-moment idea?"

I shrug. "It's no big deal. I'm not cutting it off. My hair is already dyed. If I don't like it, I'll dye it back. Besides, I'd like to see what I'd look like if I looked like me."

Okay, so maybe I'm not making the most sense I've ever made in my life, but the play's going to go on and I'm going to be in it.

Lizabett and I are the only ones left on the stage so I lift my fist in the air and bring it down with a resounding, "Yes!"

The saxophone player looks up from where he's sitting on the stage steps and plays me a very nice full note of congratulations.

Now that I see the play is going forward, I am anxious to get myself ready to play the part of Mary. I pinch myself. I can't believe it. I'm going to be Mary.

"I'll need to get one of those home dye kits," I say as Lizabett and I walk down the aisle so we can start heading back to Pasadena. "Maybe you could stop on the way home."

"Are you sure you should dye it yourself?"

I shrug. "Who else has time? Marilee is getting everything ready for the party. I don't think Randy would want to do it. And you need to track down Becca and tell her I'm going to be in a play!"

Lizabett nods. "She'd never forgive us if you went onstage and we didn't let her know. And she hasn't been answering her cell phone."

"Anyway, I'll just get a plain brown. No big deal."

"You're going to be Mary!" Lizabett squeals again like she can't keep it in.

I grin at her. I can't quite keep it in either.

It's not until Randy calls me on my cell phone while Lizabett and I are driving back to Pasadena that I realize we have a problem.

"Did you say the producers aren't coming?" Randy asks. I can hear the sounds of the kitchen in the background. "Your aunt has been calling all afternoon adding to the menu for the party because she wants to impress these producers."

"Oh. Well, maybe one of them will still come."

"Maybe?"

I nod even though Randy can't see me. "She's going to be mad if she spends all this effort on a party and there's no important people there."

"Well, the party is really for the actors," Randy says.

I grunt. "My aunt won't think so. You're not important in my aunt's book unless you're on television or in the news or—"

"Does sports news count?"

"I guess so."

"Then we're covered."

Randy doesn't tell me what his plans are, but I feel better knowing someone is sharing my worries about my family.

Chapter Fourteen

"If you give an audience a chance, they will do half your acting for you."

—Katharine Hepburn

I can't remember why I brought this quote to the Sisterhood. Maybe it's just because I always liked Katharine Hepburn. One thing I noticed when I had cancer: I found a great deal of comfort in watching old movies. I liked to see the actresses when they were in their twenties and then later when they were sixty or seventy. It's like I got to see their lives from young to old. I wasn't sure my life would go that way and it was nice to see someone who had run the full course before they died.

My mother wasn't home when I got there. I figured she was out shopping at Bristol Farms. They have the best imported fruit around and, even though they are in South Pasadena and not San Marino, that's where my mother always heads when she thinks we need groceries.

It was just as well my mother was gone. I was jumping with excitement. The lines of the play kept going through my mind as I stepped into the shower. I had four hours until showtime and I had a lot to do. Lizabett was going to come back and pick me up so we could drive down to the play together. Marilee might come with us or she might drive her own car. I know Randy will want his Jeep, so he'll drive by himself. We have it all worked out. Marilee even got one of the waitresses to oversee the delivery and set up of the food for the after-play party so everything is arranged.

The shower steams up the mirror in my bathroom, but that's okay. I don't need a mirror to towel myself off or to read the directions for the brown hair dye. It's not the heavy-duty dye; it's that wash-away kind so I can't go too wrong. I figure I'll put the dye on and then, with that plastic little cap on my head, I'll give myself a manicure. I think a nice set of French-tipped nails would look good in Mary's century, too.

Before I do my nails, however, I decide to look in my closet, just in case I have something that would be suitable for Mary to wear. I liked that dress made out of flour sacks that the first Mary actress had, but I know there's nothing like that in my closet. I do find a brown beach cover-up, though. It might look like something a migrant worker would wear. Not to the beach, of course, but it's a coarsely-woven thing with no shape to it. It looks like something that came from a potato sack instead of a flour sack, but I pull it out just in case and lay it on my bed.

I put that old flannel robe on because it won't matter if a drop of dye falls on it.

I decide to sit out on the balcony while I do my nails. My cat comes with me. It's overcast out, but if I look north I can see the snow on Mount Wilson and, since snow is giving me my big break, I want to look at it a little. It takes me longer than I expect to put the white tips on my nails and, by the time I let my nails dry and I go back inside, I see that forty minutes have passed.

I'm only supposed to keep the dye on for twenty minutes so, after I bring my cat inside, I hop right into the shower again so I can start rinsing the stuff out of my hair. I hear the door open downstairs and know my mother is back from the store.

My mother will be so excited that I'm really going to be in the play. I towel my hair off and pull my robe on so I can go tell my mother the good news.

I step into the hall and my mother turns around.

"What'd you do?" my mother says in shock. She's holding a brown bag of groceries and it slips a little.

"I got the part!"

"No, I mean with your hair. What did you do with your beautiful hair?"

My mother is looking at me like I'd shaved my hair and had a frog tattooed on my forehead.

"I dyed my hair for the play I'm going to be in—the first actress left so I'm *on!*"

"But your hair was so beautiful."

I walk over and take the grocery bag out of my mother's arms. I know she wouldn't want to bruise any imported fruit and she might do that if the bag slides any further.

"Blond hair wouldn't work for the play, Mom. There weren't any blondes in that part of the world when Jesus was born. Besides, I'm naturally a brunette."

"Your hair was chestnut. That—" my mother points to my hair "—that's not chestnut."

"I know. It's brown."

I walk down the hall and set the bag on the table at the end. When I come back, I see my mother has gone into her room and is sitting on a chair. That's where she sits and watches television, but the television is not on. She's just sitting there.

"You can come to the play if you want," I say. "Lizabett is going to pick me up. You can come with us."

"I always took you to that place on Huntington Drive to have your hair done. They were the *specialists.* That's what they called themselves."

"I know, Mom."

I miss my dad.

I go back into the bathroom and dry my hair. My mother is right. The color is not chestnut. There's no auburn in it or any blond highlights. It's just brown. Plus, I left the color on a little too long and now my hair looks dry, like it needs a deep oil conditioner just to have some shine to it.

I go into my bedroom and get dressed in the oldest pair of blue jeans I own. I do wear a little mascara, but I don't wear any other makeup. My mother is lying on her bed with her eyes closed when I check on her before going downstairs to meet Lizabett.

At the bottom of the stairs, I stop and wrap a wool scarf around my head.

Lizabett has her radio turned up and Christmas carols playing. It's just turning dark when she comes and the temperature is starting to drop. We have the windows on her car up and her heater is on low. I notice she brought the Sisterhood journal with her. It's sticking out of her purse.

There are only Christmas decorations at a few of the houses as Lizabett turns the corner to drive onto Huntington Drive. Most houses in San Marino just have poinsettias lining the driveway and don't have any outside Christmas lights unless they're tiny white ones. Everything is so understated; it's the San Marino way. I wish there was more exuberance with Christmas here. I like houses that have the twinkle lights in red, green and yellow.

Lizabett waits until she's at a stoplight and then she turns to me with a big grin. "Guess what?"

"What?"

"Becca's coming to the play."

"Really? Becca? You're sure?"

Lizabett nods and there's no denying the look of triumph on her face.

"She doesn't have to come if she has other things she needs to do," I say.

Lizabett snorts. "Like anybody has anything more important to do when one of the Sisterhood is in a play for the very first time in her whole life."

I grin. It's getting a little warm in the car so I unwrap the scarf that's been around my head.

"You did it," Lizabett says, with a glance at me as she turns onto the freeway.

"Do you think it's too brown?"

"I don't think something can be too brown. Brown is pretty much it. I think it looks like Mary's hair would have looked."

"Me, too." I sit up a little straighter.

"And the brown hair makes your eyes stand out more."

I smile at Lizabett. "It's okay. The hair is just for the play. I'll try another brown for the real thing. Maybe something like chestnut since that seems to be the color my hair used to be."

"Chestnut. That sounds pretty."

There are cars in the parking lot of the church when we get there. During the week when the play has been rehearsing, there have always been some cars. But there are definitely more now. I see Randy's Jeep.

"You're going to still sit up front, aren't you?" I ask Lizabett as we walk to the door of the church.

She holds up her cell phone. "I'm even going to take a picture of you when you take your bow, after it's all done."

"Really?" I hold the door open for Lizabett.

Lizabett nods as she walks inside. "Then I'm going to print it out and paste it in the journal. This is your big day. I'm even going to write the exact time of the play in the journal."

"If you write something in the journal, make sure you say that I couldn't have done it without your encouragement."

Lizabett grins. "Thanks."

I leave Lizabett in the front row of the audience section and start backstage to find Randy. Just before I go behind the stage, I look back and see that Lizabett has pulled the journal out of her purse and is opening it up.

This is Lizabett. I'm so excited. This is as close as I've ever come to a star in the making. I wonder if someday a reporter from *Entertainment News* will want to interview me because I was there when Carly Winston got her big break. If they do, I want to have all of the facts right. That's why I've already written down what happened this afternoon. This is going to make a great story on how Carly got discovered. The reason I know she'll be discovered is that the producer who has the reality show isn't the only producer who was going to come and watch the play. The guy who does the lights said that the bigger producer is still coming. The one who has the prime-time comedy show.

I didn't tell Carly that another producer is still coming, because I don't want her to be nervous.

I need to write down what Carly said on the drive over here, too. Someday all of that will be important. Imagine, knowing what someone like Meryl Streep said on the way to her first acting job. Stuff like that will be important for Carly's biography. I wonder who will play me if anyone ever makes a movie out of her life.

I cannot say often enough how totally cool it would be if one of us in the Sisterhood became a star!

Oh, here comes Carly. She's in costume now, but there aren't enough people in the audience yet to bother with so she just has a blanket wrapped around her.

I see Lizabett folding the journal and putting it back in her purse.

"Do you have a safety pin?" I ask. The woman doing the costumes thought she had safety pins, but she couldn't find any and Randy's shirt is missing a button. Everyone said he could go without the button, but I think Joseph would have at least been buttoned. Mary would have seen that his clothes were properly mended for the big event.

Lizabett hands me a safety pin she finds in her purse.

"Break a leg," she whispers.

"Thanks," I say as I turn to head back to the dressing area.

It's darker in the stage area than it was a few minutes ago when I walked by and the lighting man is fiddling with switches and some kind of hood thing he puts over the lights. I get a shiver just realizing that the spotlight now is going to be on me.

In the dressing area, everyone is talking.

In the past, when I've seen nativity plays, everything is so quiet. I'm beginning to wonder if it wouldn't have sounded more like this backstage area, though, with the shepherds talking to the angel and the innkeeper saying his lines to anyone who would listen.

"Lizabett had a safety pin," I say to Randy as I offer it to him.

"Thanks," he says as he takes it.

I notice Randy looks a little nervous. Maybe that's why he hasn't mentioned my hair.

"I'm glad you agreed to play Joseph tonight," I say to him.

Randy nods. "The show must go on."

"And you do know all of the lines."

"Yeah." Randy takes a deep breath. "I just need to keep my mind on the goal."

I think he means something warm and spiritual.

"I've been in tighter spots than this in games," Randy adds, letting me know it's probably football he has on his mind.

I shrug. Football is okay. I'm sure Joseph didn't walk all that way to Bethlehem thinking lofty thoughts, either. He probably wondered how long the journey would take and whether or not they would pass anyone they knew and whether their supplies would last.

And Mary was probably wondering what it would be like to have her first baby. The needs of daily life would have been with them on that trip. They might have even gotten tired and quarreled with each other just like other couples might do. Mary might have even wondered if Joseph liked the new way she was wearing her hair.

The director comes in and he gives us a pep talk, telling us that it's important that we each play our role. He looks better than he did this afternoon when both of his lead actors left, but he's still a little quieter than usual.

"Just do your best," the director finally says in conclusion. "We've got five minutes to the curtain."

Just then I see the door to the dressing area is open and a couple of athletic-looking guys are standing there.

"Hey, man," Randy says as he leaves my side and goes over to slap the two men on the shoulder. "I wasn't sure you could make it."

"Are you kidding?" one of them says. "You call us and we're here. We've got your back. We wouldn't miss it."

Randy has a wide grin on his face and he waves the two men inside. "Come meet my leading lady. This is Carly," Randy says as he walks the two men over to me. "She's getting ready to play Mary."

"So you're playing opposite him?" one of the guys asks me.

"Sure am," I say.

"She's all in costume already," Randy says as we're all standing there. "She even dyed her hair for tonight. She's usually a blonde."

"Well, you're going all out," the guy who hasn't spoken yet says. "Impressive."

I nod and try to keep my smile in place.

"Two minutes to the curtain," the director calls out. "Time to get in place."

"Hey, we'll see you afterward," the first guy says and they both turn to leave.

I wonder if Mary was ever disappointed in Joseph. I wonder if he ever wanted to show off Mary to his friends and, in doing so, let her know that he was bragging about an image of her that wasn't even true.

"My hair really is brown," I say to Randy as we turn to walk toward the stage.

Randy is looking down at his shirt, however. "That pin just stuck me."

"Take it out if you need to," I say.

We're on the stage. The sound of the saxophone is growing louder and the lights on the other side of the curtain are starting to go dim.

Randy looks like he manages to snap the safety pin into place. Then he surprises me. He bends down and gives me a quick kiss right on the lips. My face is still rosy when the curtain opens on us just standing there.

Chapter Fifteen

"The loneliest woman in the world is a woman without a close woman friend."

—*George Santayana*

Becca brought this quote to a Sisterhood meeting when we were partially through our treatments. She was intense about everything and friendship was important to her. She's the one who always made sure the Sisterhood was well and healthy. Back then, I sometimes thought we kept going because of her sheer will to see us make it through together. With her, there was no looking back. I used to think that she might be saving our lives back then. I know it wasn't true; she didn't do anything medical. But it felt like it all the same.

We are onstage. It is the moment for the play to begin. And then I see Becca. She is sitting beside

Lizabett and she gives me a quiet thumbs-up. I give her a smile that comes from the center of my being. She is here.

And then Randy clears his throat and the play begins.

Randy and I have our lines down like we were born knowing these roles. The first scene takes place in a weathered old house. Dust and barren landscape show out the window.

Joseph is talking with Mary's father while Mary wanders back to a corner of the room. There is a small Christmas tree and Mary sits beside it. There is a crèche under the tree and Mary picks up the ceramic figures, clearly daydreaming about them. The spotlight shows a silhouette of the Biblical nativity scene on the wall behind Mary and the saxophonist plays a melancholy tune.

Because the main action is taking place in the middle of the Great Depression, the talk between the men on the side of the stage is of crops that are failing and money that is due to the bank. A wedding ring is quietly mentioned by the younger man, but it's clear that it had been ordered and then returned.

Mary looks up at the mention of the ring and then back at the crèche in her hands. The silhouette of the nativity scene changes on the wall behind her.

I know the Mary of the Bible didn't have a wedding ring, but I wonder whether she had the usual things a young girl had to celebrate her newly married life back then. There was no marriage feast mentioned for her. I wondered earlier, when I read about the wedding feast that had Jesus turning the water to wine at his mother's request, if Mary was so intent on seeing someone else's wedding feast go well because she hadn't had one of her own.

I'm a little surprised at how holy the play starts to feel. I know it's a first attempt by a young playwright, but it has deep feeling in it. A miracle occurred thousands of years ago and this play shows how the ordinary people who were there might have felt at the time.

Before I know it, intermission is here.

The curtain closes and I look at Randy.

"We're doing it," he says.

"Good work," the director says from behind us. "Be sure and get a drink before you go on again. You'll get thirsty in the second half if you don't."

There's a gap in the curtain at the edge of the stage and I see a quick glimpse of Lizabett as I walk backstage. She has her head bent down and I suspect she's writing in the Sisterhood journal. I wonder what she's saying.

Hi, this is Lizabett. I never knew this play was so powerful. I've sat through many of the rehearsals, but there's an intensity to this performance that was missing in the rehearsals. I think it is Carly's acting. And, to be fair, they never had the silhouettes on the wall in the rehearsals. These keep reminding the audience of the Biblical story even as the actors show the Depression-era story. It is like a play within a play within a play kind of a thing.

That would be a good quote if someone is ever reading this to get information because they're doing a biography of the famous actress, Carly Winston.

I know Becca is impressed. Her eyes didn't leave the stage when the play was going on. The only reason she isn't sitting here beside me now is because she had to use the restroom.

Before the intermission is over, I need to describe the stage and the costumes a little more. I know a copy of the script will survive, but no one will know twenty years from now what everything looked like.

The house in the first scene looks like whoever lived there had been poor for a long time. Fine crack lines went through the yellowed paint on the wall. Nothing matched. The sofa was brown and worn. A navy throw blanket was draped over the back of the sofa. The small Formica table in the corner had three mismatched chairs sitting under it. One of the chairs had its back broken.

The whole house would have to improve to be considered a fixer-upper.

The costumes, of course, were also threadbare. It looked like there had been some kind of print at one time on Mary's dress, but the color had faded until it was all just an uneven beige. All of the shoes, even Mary's, were scuffed and looked like they'd been worn by someone who was plowing a field. Joseph wore patched overalls and a battered straw hat.

All of the costumes looked like they had seen more than their share of sweat and dust.

In contrast, the silhouettes of the nativity scene that are being shown on the walls look so peaceful. For the first time, I'm sort of getting the point of the play. Most of us have often looked at the nativity scene in such a spiritual way that we've forgotten that Mary and Joseph were flesh and blood like us. Their feet had to hurt after a long day's walk and their journey hadn't been one of ease and luxury. They might have had money troubles just like the Depression-era Mary and Joseph.

Someone just dimmed the lights so the intermission is almost over. I look up as I see the actors file past the gap in the curtain at the edge of the stage. I give a smile to Carly and I think she sees me.

I never knew an intermission could go so quickly. I was glad to see Lizabett, though, and I saw Becca walking down the aisle so all is well. I put some hairspray on my hair, because I ride in the back of the pickup in the next scene and I don't want my hair to bounce. I also readjusted the pillow under my dress so that I'll continue to look pregnant. Then I drank half a bottle of water because this dusty look is making me thirsty.

The curtain opens again, and we're on our way. By now, Randy and I are leaving the old farmhouse with a table and two chairs and some suitcases in the back of this pickup. We only have a couple of scenes, though, before the pickup breaks down and we are forced to hitchhike to where we're going.

According to the script, we're being forced to travel because of a special kind of census that the government is taking. There is a lot of grumbling about the government in the script, but no one seems to be willing to ignore the census.

We are able to get a ride in the back of someone's old pickup. There are also several cages of live chickens in the back of the pickup; we only have a cardboard suitcase with us. As we ride, there's a silhouette on the stage behind us that shows Mary and Joseph crossing the desert. Mary is riding on a donkey.

The back of the pickup is really just a big prop and it vibrates to indicate that we are moving. I've been on the vibrating pickup in rehearsals, but this is the first time that the live chickens have been here with us. There is enough squawking going on that it's hard for Randy and me to get our lines out.

The chickens are also flapping their feathers and Randy sneezes. Twice.

"Bless you," I say without thinking. Then I notice that the safety pin that's supposed to hold his shirt together is unhooked and will poke him if nothing is done so I reach over and hook it for him. It's the kind of thing Mary would have done for her Joseph.

"Thanks," Randy says with a grin as he gives me a quick kiss on the forehead.

I hear a sigh in the audience and I know it has

never occurred to someone out there before that Mary might be fond of her Joseph.

Soon night is starting to fall onstage and the pickup comes to a stop. There are snow flurries falling. Mary and Joseph are in the town that represents Bethlehem and they get down from the back of the pickup with their suitcase and look around them.

It is a small town and it's crowded with people. Everyone has their arms wrapped around themselves for warmth. Joseph points to the flashing Motel 6 sign and he and Mary start to walk toward it. The sidewalk is crowded with people and there are fires burning in a couple of cut-down trash cans. People are gathered around the fires with their hands outstretched.

The desk clerk at the Motel 6 shakes his head and points to the No Vacancy sign before he relents and tells Joseph that the restroom in the gas station across the street is always open. There's a hallway that the restroom as well and it would have room for a pallet. His brother owns the gas station and won't mind if Joseph and Mary use the two rooms for the night.

When Joseph says they have no blankets, the clerk gives him a short stack of folded, clean towels.

"I wish it could be more," the clerk says. "But at least the area there is heated. It's going to be a cold night this close to Christmas."

The clerk points to a blinking snowman that sits in the lobby of the motel.

Joseph takes the towels and he and Mary head over to the gas station.

Throughout this section of the play, a series of silhouettes showing Mary and Joseph in the real Bethlehem two thousand years ago is displayed on the stage walls behind the actors.

It is easy for me to pretend to be Mary by now. I know how everything is going to go. I already see the shepherds gathered around one of the fires as Randy and I walk across the stage to the gas station.

The hallway leading to the restroom is wide and clean. The desk clerk was right that there is a place to set up a bed of sorts that would be a little out of the way. If nothing else it will be warm.

The saxophonist has moved into a musical selection that is a little impatient now.

I think that must be how women feel who are about to give birth. I suspect Mary felt the same way.

The stage wall of the gas station is clear. It makes a good place for the silhouettes to be projected and there are now scenes of Mary and Joseph in the manger behind Randy and me.

I like the feeling that the Biblical Mary and Joseph are following Randy and I around as we represent them in this play. I feel serene just thinking about Mary doing some of the same things that I am doing. She and Joseph must have made a bed out of straw just like we are making one out of old towels.

There are a few empty cardboard boxes in one corner of the hallway and a calendar on the wall with the month of December 1937 showing.

The spotlight in the play cuts to the scene on the other side of the stage with the shepherds standing by the trash-can fires. Now that the light isn't so intense on me, I can look out in the audience and actually see things.

I notice Marilee is seated several rows behind Lizabett and Becca. She must have been here all along; I just didn't know where to look for her as I glanced through the curtain during the intermission. I look around and also see the two friends of Randy's who came: the ones who think I'm really a blonde.

I don't understand guys. I admit that right off. I thought Randy liked *me* and wasn't so interested in whether or not I had a certain blond look. He sure didn't sound like it when he was introducing me to his friends, though. Of course, I might be misreading him. I could just be overly sensitive because of my mother's reaction. Maybe it's mothers I don't understand.

I know my mother's not out in the audience, but I can't help but look for her anyway. It's so different than it was when I was competing to be the Rose Parade Queen. My mother was at every little judging event they had. Nothing would have kept her away from the main event. Of course, I had become a blonde for the competition and I think my mother was looking at that competition and my new blondness as a way to show that she, my father and I belonged in a place like San Marino.

I don't think I won the Rose Queen crown because I was a blonde, but I suspect my mother believes that, even though there's no rational reason for it as many of the queens have been brunettes. I wish now that I had tried to win the competition looking like myself.

The spotlight is still on the shepherds talking by the fire when there is the wail of a new baby that's just been born. The shepherds all look up and then see the angel standing beside them. The angel is dressed in spotless white and towers over them. They clearly think they're seeing something supernatural and they start to move away. Well, run really.

"Don't worry," the angel commands in a deep voice. "I won't harm you. I have good news for you. Nearby, a baby was born of a virgin. He is the Messiah."

The shepherds stop running and a couple of them fall to their knees.

The angel shakes his head. "Don't worship me. The baby born tonight is the one you should worship. Listen and I'll tell you how to find Him."

While the light is on the angel, I wiggle the pillow out of my costume and Randy slips it behind a stage wall at the same time as someone brings in a doll and sets it up in one of the cardboard boxes that had been in the corner of this hallway. The doll is wrapped in a towel.

By the time the light swings back to Randy and me, I am kneeling by the baby's box and so is Randy. We have arranged ourselves as much as possible to match the silhouette behind us of the real nativity scene.

The street noise outside has been muffled and we only know the shepherds are standing outside the open doorway when one of them clears his throat. Randy tells them to come in and see the baby if they'd like.

The outside noise completely fades away now and the saxophonist plays "What Child Is This." The shepherds stare at the doll in the box and don't shuffle their feet like they have previously in rehearsals.

We all know we're pretending, of course, but I feel that we're all thinking about what we would have been feeling now if this were the real nativity scene. The silhouettes on the wall behind us keep reminding us that something amazing happened two thousand years ago to humble people in an even more humble place.

The wise men come into the scene at the end, looking like the rock stars they are supposed to be. They don't have crowns, but they have rhinestones on their shirts and gold fringes on their pants. They've got bags of gold in their hands and guitars strapped to their backs.

The silhouette behind us changes slightly to include the three crowned figures and the light fades as the play comes to an end.

The curtain closes and there is a full minute of silence. I look at Randy and he looks at me. Surely, someone would clap just to be polite.

"Were we that bad?" he whispers.

Then applause erupts from out front. People are stomping their feet and a few of them give piercing whistles.

"I don't think so," I whisper back to Randy with a grin on my face. I wouldn't have wanted to let Mary down and I suspect Randy feels the same about Joseph.

The curtain opens and the whole cast goes forward to take a bow. Then it's just Randy and I, holding hands, bowing in front of the audience.

The applause is deafening.

Then someone from beside the stage walks up and hands me a huge bouquet of roses. There are more roses in this bouquet than in the one I got when I was crowned queen of the Rose Court.

"I didn't know they were doing this," I say to Randy.

"They didn't," he says. "They're from me."

"Oh." I'm already smiling so wide I don't think I can smile any bigger, but I am wrong. "Thank you. They're beautiful."

"It's what Joseph would have done," Randy says quietly. "For his Mary."

Okay, so now I'm beyond smiling. I think I'm crying, just a little.

Chapter Sixteen

"Don't let yesterday use up too much of today."

—Will Rogers

Rose brought us this quote when we were all on the mend. It was her way of reminding us that we needed to look forward and not backward. We were just beginning to see that we actually still had lives ahead of us. There was an exuberant feeling in the Sisterhood the night Rose brought us that quote. We knew things were going to be more hopeful the day after we talked about that quote.

There haven't been all that many moments of sheer joy in my life and taking my bows on Mary's behalf has definitely been one of them. Randy escorts me down off the stage and we make our way down the aisle so we can shake hands with everyone as they leave. This was the director's idea and it is a good one. Everyone seems to want to say something to either Mary or Joseph.

I am carrying my bouquet of roses in one arm, but I still have one hand free for shaking hands with others. The roses are deep red, scented ones and the smell surrounds me.

Mostly, people want to congratulate me on doing so well in the play, but some of the people have more personal things to say. One elderly woman takes my hand and holds it for the longest time as she tells me about the time when she'd been Mary in a church Christmas play as a youngster. She says it started her on a lifelong journey of faith and that she hopes it does the same for me.

I tell her I hope it does, too, and I mean it. I pull one of the roses out of my bouquet and give it to her. She beams as she carries it off with her.

Then Becca comes to shake my hand.

"Forgive me," she says. Her chin is determined and her eyes are steady. "I was wrong to be so angry."

I know what an apology like that costs Becca.

"I was wrong, too," I say. "I never should have let you keep believing I was richer than I was. I should have said something."

Becca grins. "I don't know why I kept believing it, anyway. You're the only one of us who doesn't have a car. I guess I always thought a chauffeur was dropping you off."

"A chauffer called the city bus," I say.

"I know." Becca takes a deep breath. "I think I

was always a little jealous of you for having everything so easy. And then, to find out it hadn't been that way at all, I felt like a fool."

I shake my head. "It wasn't you. It was me."

"We'll talk about it later," Becca says.

The line stretches on behind her and I can see Marilee is anxious to say hello to me.

Several other people give me their regards before Marilee gets to me.

"Did you *see* those guys?" Marilee says in awe. "The ones with Randy."

I knew it. "Quinn is working tonight so you're out looking at other men. I don't even know if they're single."

"Those aren't other men. They're Dodgers baseball players. I've got to get their autographs. My dad would be so excited. I want something special to add to his Christmas gift and this could be it. Did you meet them?"

"Randy introduced us before the play, but I didn't know they were professional athletes." So this was his answer to my aunt's desire to have some important people at the party. Pro baseball players will make my aunt very happy.

Marilee looks at me like I'm hopeless. "One of them hit a ton of home runs last season. Don't you read the newspaper?"

"Not the sports section."

Marilee looks behind her and sees there are several people still waiting. "Put in a good word with Randy for me. I'll try to find something for them to autograph. You don't happen to have a baseball at your house, do you?"

I shake my head. "My uncle has some golf balls."

"That will never do. I'll ask Lizabett. Maybe she has something in her car they could autograph. You're going right over to the party at your uncle's, aren't you?"

I nod. "I'm hitching a ride with Lizabett and she's going right over."

Marilee shakes her head. "Didn't Randy ask you to drive over with him?"

"No, we haven't really had much of a chance to talk. We've been onstage."

Marilee nods. "He'll ask you. That'll give you time to ask him about his Dodgers friends. And find out if he carries a baseball in that Jeep of his."

It takes a little longer for the line to wind down. The director is the last one through and he stops to get the address for my uncle's house. The party will already be going before any of us get there.

Marilee is right. As soon as the director walks away, Randy comes over and asks me to ride to the party with him. I tell him I need to let Lizabett know so I walk over and give her a quick hug so she can be going as well.

Lizabett was putting the Sisterhood journal back in her purse as I walk over.

"Did you write something?"

She shakes her head. "I was just reading what Becca wrote."

Lizabett pulls the journal out of her purse and hands it to me. "Read it when you get a chance."

I take the journal although I can't take anything else now since I already have the roses in one arm.

I walk back to Randy and we walk out to his Jeep together. I kind of miss the silhouette of Mary and Joseph following us around.

"Thanks for everything," I say. "If you hadn't agreed to fill in at the last minute, there wouldn't have been a play."

"Oh, the director would have thought of something."

"Yeah, me reading Joseph's lines in a deep voice and Mary's lines in another."

It's cozy driving down the freeway back to Pasadena. I've put my roses in the backseat and they make the whole Jeep smell nice. I wonder what Randy's friends will think if they drive somewhere with him soon.

Which reminds me. I tell Randy that Marilee noticed his fans were baseball players and she would like an autograph on something.

He, of course, graciously agrees to ask them if they'll sign something.

"You don't have a baseball with you, do you?" I ask.

I can see there's nothing in his Jeep except for

his snorkeling gear and I don't think Marilee's father wants an autograph on a black fin.

Randy shakes his head. "Maybe one of the guys will have a baseball with him though. I'll ask them."

I think about asking Randy what he thinks about my new hair color. It seems a little odd to just blurt out a question like that, though, so I try to think of a way to ease into it.

"I noticed Becca was there," Randy says.

I nod. "It was good to see her. We've made our peace."

"I thought so."

It seems like it takes no time at all before we are turning onto Huntington Drive. We'll be at my uncle's house in a few minutes.

"I hope they found a bowl for the spiced cider. It's cold enough tonight people will want something warm."

Randy turns onto my uncle's street. "Marilee asked Linda to take care of everything and she's very responsible. I'm sure everything's perfect."

Randy hasn't met my aunt yet so I don't tell him that perfection might not be so easy to attain in the house we're heading toward. Of course, having some big-name baseball players among the guests will help.

I see the lights of my uncle's house while we're still down the block. There are lights in every single window and lots of twinkle lights spreading out to the lawn. Christmas music is floating out from the house. That's when I notice a figure in a light-colored garment wandering around on the lawn.

"That's my mother!"

I look again. "In my old bathrobe."

And, it's light enough with all of the Christmas decorations going that the neighbors on all sides could see her.

"She hates that bathrobe," I say as Randy parks his Jeep at the curb in front of my uncle's house.

"Maybe she lost something," Randy says.

I don't tell him that my mother would need to lose her mind before she would willingly start wandering around San Marino in that old flannel bathrobe. She doesn't even go outside without makeup on. Not even when she's sick. She can't stand the thought of the neighbors saying something.

"Mom, what's wrong?" I say after I get out of the Jeep and run over to her.

My mother looks up at me and I can see she has been crying. "I lost your cat. I left the door open and she ran outside. I've looked, but I can't find her. You love that cat."

"I love you more, Mom," I say as I give her shoulders a squeeze. "You shouldn't be out here in the cold. Marie will come inside before we know it. It's just all of these people around tonight."

I turn my mother toward the house and we're walking back together.

Randy is almost behind us so I turn around

and mouth at him. "Marie's loose. Can you find her again?"

Randy is the one who convinced my cat to come back home the last time she ran away.

Randy leaves on his mission and I keep walking with my mother.

"I just keep losing things," my mother mutters as we get to the stairs leading up to our rooms in the house. "Nobody wants to live with me anymore."

"Don't worry about Marie," I say again as I open the door. "She'll be back. Of course she wants to live here with us."

"Your dad doesn't," my mother says as she steps in the door.

Okay, so now I know my mother has really been worrying. I should have woken her up earlier and insisted she come to the play with me. Maybe if she saw me with my brown hair playing the role of Mary and everybody being so happy with the play, she could have adjusted to the change.

"Dad is in a rehab center," I say gently. "He'll come back when he's well enough. You know that."

My mother and I are inside our little stairwell now and she turns to me.

"I should have told you. He's been out of the rehab center for months now. He refuses to come back and live with us."

"Oh."

There's a dim light in the stairwell, but I don't

need to see my mother's face to know she's telling me the absolute truth.

"He says he won't live in my brother's house anymore. That it makes him want to drink. That he can't be a man living off someone's charity like this."

I feel a moment's panic. "But Dad has to be somewhere. Where is he if he's not at the rehab center?"

"He got a job at the mall and rented a place in Eagle Rock. Eagle Rock!"

Okay, so Eagle Rock isn't San Marino. In fact, it's twenty steps or so down from San Marino. Maybe even fifty steps down. But it's not like my dad has been living on the moon for the past few months. It can't be more then ten miles away from here.

"But why haven't we seen him?"

"He comes by when you're in school. We didn't want to upset you."

Now I have to sit down on the stairs.

"I know how attached you are to San Marino," my mother says. "We can't afford to live here unless we stay in your uncle's house. And you deserve to be in San Marino. This is where you belong. Your dad will just have to stay in Eagle Rock and visit us when he can."

"No, Mom," I say as I look up at her. "I don't *need* to be anywhere. What I need is for my parents to be honest with me."

My mother draws the flannel robe closer around her. "You say that now, but there'll come a day when you'll regret it if we leave."

"Why? Why would you think that?"

My mother frowns. "Well, anyone would, dear. You've been the Rose Queen. Your dad and I can't expect you to sleep on the sofa of his one-bedroom apartment."

"Then I can get my own apartment," I say. "I've been hoping to move after Christmas anyway."

My mother stares at me like I've grown wings right in front of her eyes.

"I'm old enough to live on my own," I say to her softly.

"But you've been sick. The Hodgkin's disease—"

I smile. "I'll be fine. I can't live my life wrapped in cotton. I have to grow up sometime."

I follow my mom up the stairway.

"Does this mean Dad will be here for Christmas?" I say when we reach the top.

"I guess so," my mother says with a smile of her own. "I'm worried about him being all alone in that apartment on Christmas day."

The color in my mother's face is looking better.

"Why don't you get dressed and come down to the party?" I say to my mom. "We made all kinds of wonderful appetizers and there's eggnog and spiced cider."

"I've been smelling the cider. And I think your cat smelled some of the other food."

"Well, then," I say. "She won't be hard to find. She'll be hanging around the doorways begging for a treat."

My mother goes to her room to get dressed and I remember the roses I left in Randy's Jeep. I go back down the stairs and I see Randy holding Marie and talking to his two baseball friends that have arrived.

The two friends are walking into the house by the time I reach Randy.

"You found her," I say.

Randy nods as he pets my cat. "I think she decided to give up easy this time. She knows I'd just get her in the end anyway."

"I forgot my roses, too," I say.

Randy reaches into a pocket and gives me a key. "I'll take your cat back to your doorway."

I nod. "I left the door unlocked. Just set her at the bottom of the stairs and she'll be fine."

"One of us better go inside and check on the food, too," Randy says. "I'll do that after I put Marie inside."

There are so many lights around I don't need to fumble to get the key into the door of Randy's Jeep. I smile when I see the roses and then I remember that I have the Sisterhood journal as well.

I take the roses upstairs and fill several vases with them before I take the Sisterhood journal into my bedroom.

Marie is curled up in the basket in the corner of my room, but she's not sleeping so I turn the light on higher. I want to know what Becca wrote in the Sisterhood journal.

* * *

Hi, this is Becca. I never knew my ideals could get me into so much trouble. I've always known I like things to be black and white, right and wrong. But I didn't know there could be so much gray in life at the same time.

I think when we all had cancer I needed to know things were black and white. If I admitted to gray, I was admitting to the possibility of death.

I don't know why I put Carly up on some kind of a pedestal. I used to look at her when we were meeting and think, if I could only be like her, I would live. No one that serene could possibly die.

Carly was our golden girl with everything handed to her and I felt like I was the tomboy who had to keep scrapping along just to keep what she had in life. I sometimes went home from meetings wondering what I could do to be more like Carly. Was it some kind of designer brand for my clothes? A certain way of walking? I even tried on a blond wig in a store once until I realized blond hair made me look even sicker than I was.

The problem with having Carly on a pedestal is that I failed to be a very good friend to her.

I'm sorry, Carly.

That's all I have to say. I hope you still want to be my friend.

I had a tear in my eye when I finished reading what Becca had written in the journal. The truth is that I used to envy Becca, too. She always seemed so in control of her future and I was floundering. Even without the Hodgkin's disease I would have been adrift. But Becca always seemed so sure that she knew the way.

I need to go downstairs and give her a hug.

I stop in the bathroom and take a brush to my hair. It definitely needs a conditioner. No wonder Randy hasn't complimented me on it. I try pulling it back, but it's too thick. I give up and put some silver dangling earrings on. A little jewelry might help take the focus off my hair.

Chapter Seventeen

"What is a weed? A plant whose virtues have not yet been discovered."

—Ralph Waldo Emerson

Rose liked to bring quotes like this to the Sisterhood. She kept trying to make us realize that there was so much room for hope in the world. Looking back, I think she also might have wanted us to be kinder in our judgments of other people. All too often, we looked at others and at ourselves critically. That's not a good way to begin any friendship. Rose was the one who had faith in all of us that we could be good friends to each other. She saw our potential. We are forever indebted to her for that. I know she'll be happy, but not surprised, that Becca is back with us.

I smell cinnamon when I knock on my uncle's door. I also hear the sounds of laughter and talking.

Someone yells, "Come in," and I open the door to one of those scenes I used to visualize through the French doors in The Pews. Everyone just radiates goodwill and Christmas cheer. Maybe part of it is relief that opening night is over and went well, but the mood feels good whatever it is. There is an abundance of smiles and well wishes.

I recognize a couple of the kitchen helpers from The Pews and they are passing around huge trays of appetizers. There are the stuffed mushrooms and the bacon-wrapped chestnuts, along with sliced imported cheese and rose-curled radishes. The trays look like they could be photographed for a gourmet food magazine.

And the drinks. There's a table set up on one side of the room that has big bowls of eggnog and fruit punch. Whipped cream floats in the eggnog bowl and orange slices swirl around in the bowl of fruit punch. I see Thermos jugs that must hold the hot spiced cider that I have been smelling.

The cast members are having a good time. I see some shepherds bragging about being the ones who were in charge of the fire. The fact that it was a fake fire does not seem to deter them; they are making it sound like the fires would have gone out if they hadn't kept piling the wood on them. And, if the fire had gone out, the play would have been over because the shepherds would have all gone home early.

Marilee sees me and comes over. "Thank you.

Thank you. Thank you. Randy introduced me to *them.* I even got their autographs."

"Did you find a baseball for them to sign?"

Marilee shakes her head and then gleefully holds up her prize, a round silver ornament. "Your aunt gave me this off of her Christmas tree and Becca had a permanent marker in her purse so voilà—it's done."

Marilee spins the ornament around and I see all the writing on it.

"The guys didn't just sign it, they wished my dad a merry Christmas and made it all very personal. They even mentioned me. It'll be perfect. I'm going to tie a red bow around it and he can hang it on his tree. It'll be better than one of those keepsake ornaments. My dad told me he was going to have a tree this year since Quinn and I and my mom are going over to his place for a while on Christmas day."

"Your mom, too?"

Marilee nods. "Just for a few hours. Not that anything has changed between them. That's why I didn't say anything to the Sisterhood earlier. I wasn't sure one of them wouldn't pull out."

That reminds me. "I need to tell you about my dad in our next meeting, too."

"Only if it feels right," Marilee says. "We really don't need to tell each other everything."

"That's good because it's going to take me a while to know what's up before I'll even know what to say."

Marilee looks at me quizzically.

"I'm not keeping secrets. I just don't know much yet."

Marilee nods. "I know how that is. Sometimes people surprise you."

"Speaking of which, I can't believe my aunt gave you one of her ornaments."

Every year, my aunt has her Christmas trees professionally decorated. She doesn't even let my uncle touch the ornaments once they're on the tree. It's not that the ornaments are so expensive, it's that they're placed just so.

Marilee grins. "When she heard what I needed, she reached right over to the tree and took one off for me."

Marilee dangles another signed ornament in front of me. This one is gold and signed in black marker as well.

"Of course, she pulled this one off, too, and asked me to get it signed at the same time. She thought it was a great gift idea."

"But my uncle doesn't play baseball. He golfs. I don't think he even watches baseball on television."

"It's not for your uncle. It's for the housekeeper's son."

I didn't think my aunt even knew little Manny. The housekeeper only brought him around when she absolutely couldn't find anyone to stay with him. Manny was ten years old and sat in the kitchen when he came over. I knew him, of course, because I always stopped by the kitchen door on my way upstairs so I could pick up any scraps that the housekeeper had left over from dinner the night before. I use them to feed my cat.

My aunt thought housekeeper was a more dignified title than cook so she called Mrs. Gonzales that even though the woman's duties primarily include preparing breakfast, lunch and dinner for my aunt and uncle.

I never would have guessed my aunt had a soft spot in her whole heart. Which just shows me, I shouldn't assume people can't change. Rose was right all along about people being able to change. My mother is changing. My dad sounds like he's changed. I am changing. There's no reason my aunt can't change right along with us.

Speaking of people changing, here comes Becca.

I open my arms when I see her and she comes right to me.

"I'm sorry," I say as I hug her.

"Not as sorry as I am," she says.

We look at each other and it's like we've never been apart.

When Becca walks away, I look around and see Randy setting up a small table by the door that goes into the kitchen area. He sees me and, after he has spread a white cloth on the table, he walks over. "That will make it easier for the waiters. They won't have to keep hauling the empty glasses back one at a time."

I'm proud that Randy thinks of other people even at a party like this.

"Is there something I need to be doing?" I ask because I would like to be someone who thinks of others as well.

Randy shakes his head. "You've already done enough. This is a great place to have a party."

I start to explain that my aunt and uncle are really doing it for the director, not for me. But after Marilee's ornament, I'm not so sure. Maybe they have more fondness for me than I know.

Randy is still looking around. I forget he's never been inside my uncle's house.

"It's my aunt's mission in life to have rooms like these," I say.

And it's true. My aunt spends a small fortune when she remodels one of the downstairs rooms. Everything coordinates without matching anything exactly. The ornate green pattern of one sofa becomes a counterpoint to a nearby chair that has a different pattern but colors that blend. My aunt's interior designer has to hunt for days for the combinations that my aunt finally settles on buying.

In fairness I need to add to what I've said, though. "My aunt isn't all about the looks of it, though. I think she's changing. She gave Marilee an ornament so she could have your friends sign it."

"Yeah, I heard."

"You don't know what a miracle that is. Especially since my aunt had another one autographed for her housekeeper's young son. If my aunt can change, I guess anyone can change."

Randy nods. "I have sure seen some changes in my life."

This is not the opening I'd been looking for, but it might be the best opening I'm going to get to talk about the changes I want to make. But, before I can say anything, someone is clanking a spoon against a glass and calling for everyone's attention.

The director is motioning for everyone to come closer to the center of the one room and we obligingly crowd together.

"I want to say thank you," the director says. Someone must have given him a portable microphone, because his voice is clear through to the back of the room. "I had my moments of doubt that this play would go on at the last minute, but you have all pulled us through."

There is applause.

"I want you to know I'm proud of each of you," the director continues and there is more applause.

"And I want to read you some words from our first review. It'll be coming out tomorrow, but remember you heard it here first."

Everyone is quiet as the director unfolds the paper he has in his hands.

"Despite a last-minute casting crisis, this was an exceptionally well-acted performance. Mary and Joseph transported us back to the days of the Dust Bowl and, in doing that, they showed us the wonder of the first Christmas in a fresh, new way. It's community theatre, but it rivals the big productions when it comes to heart."

The director calls for quiet when people start applauding.

"Before you wear your hands out, let's give it up for our very own Mary and Joseph. It's not every Mary who will dye her hair to play the part."

At that, everyone starts to clap their hands. I see my mother has just slipped in the door and she is beaming at me.

Randy and I smile and nod in every direction. I am prouder than I was when someone put that Rose Queen crown on my head years ago.

Only one thing bothers me.

"That's not why I dyed my hair," I murmur in an aside to Randy.

I guess I say it with enough feeling that Randy turns to look at me. "I don't get it. What's wrong your hair?"

By now, the applause has stopped and everyone is chatting again.

Randy is still looking at me.

"It's my very *brown* hair."

"But it's only dye. You can change it back if you want."

"Is that what you want?" I say, feeling miserable. "Some guys prefer the blond look."

"Not me. I like you just the way you are."

"Well, I don't think I will keep it quite this

brown," I say, a little happier now. "My real color is more of a chestnut color and not as dry, of course."

"I don't care if you dye your hair green," Randy says emphatically. "I'm not smitten with you because of your hair."

"Really?"

"Of course not. How shallow do you think I am?"

"No, I mean the part about you being smitten."

At the moment, even I wouldn't care if my hair was green.

"Can't you tell?" Randy grins. "I took you to brunch at the Ritz-Carlton and bought you a dozen and a half long-stem red roses. Who did you think I was trying to impress?"

"My mother."

Randy laughs at that. "Well, maybe I was a little. Your mother seems to have definite opinions about what a guy should do to show he is worthy of dating you."

"My mother and I don't always agree. Next time we can go to a little Thai place instead of the Ritz-Carlton."

"And the roses?"

"I like the roses. They can stay."

Randy laughs as he puts his arm around me and gives me a quick kiss on the lips. "You got a deal."

"Oh," I say. "And if my mother tries to tell you that I shouldn't work a day in my life, don't listen to her. I intend to have a job soon. I don't want to be a princess anymore."

Randy's eyes are starting to do their crinkling thing and I'm not sure he's even been really listening to me, but then he answers. "You got it."

This time the kiss Randy gives me isn't so quick. It would have lasted longer if people hadn't noticed he was kissing me and started to applaud.

"Half of them think we're together like Mary and Joseph," I say as we pull apart.

"The fans are never wrong," Randy says in my ear as he kisses me again.

I'm inclined to agree.

Chapter Eighteen

"In the faces of men and women I see God."
—*Walt Whitman*

I think I'm the one who brought this quote to the Sisterhood. After being sick for a while, I became struck with people's faces. The face of a sick person doesn't hide much to those who look at it closely. Back then, I thought to see many problems in the faces around me. I never thought to see God in someone's face though. I knew I saw kindness in Rose's face, but that was as far as I went.

This is Carly and I'm sitting in our back room at The Pews. I'm writing in the Sisterhood journal while I'm waiting for the others to come to the meeting tonight. It is the Thursday night after Christmas and I've neglected the journal for almost a week now.

That's why I'm catching up. I know Lizabett has written a lot of nonsense about me being discovered as a movie star, but my one performance is over and no movie producer has called me. I haven't told Lizabett, but I'm not even disappointed.

I don't think being a movie star would be good for me right now.

I've decided to become a Christian. Not that it means I couldn't also be a movie star. But it does mean that I have other things I need to focus on in my life for the time being. I've met with Pastor Engstrom and he's going to meet with me for a few weeks in January so that I can learn a little more about the Bible.

I think Randy is going to meet with Pastor Engstrom, too, but we are doing it separately. We don't want to be distracted by each other.

I'm glad we're doing it that way. I really like Randy and it's difficult to think about much else when he's around. And, Marilee, when you read this, you can say you told me so. I know you did. You were right.

Randy will always be my Joseph.

The day after the big party was the day before Christmas Eve and I went shopping. After Randy and I talked about Mary and Joseph at the party, I knew exactly what I wanted to get for Randy.

I bought him a small crèche, carved out of olive wood. I knew he didn't have one, because he said he didn't usually even decorate for Christmas. He didn't have a tree or ornaments or anything.

He loved his crèche when I gave it to him. The face of Joseph even looked a little like Randy's face.

Christmas day was wonderful. Randy, my mother and I all went to my dad's new place in Eagle Rock. It was so good to see my dad again. And he is doing just fine. His place is not large or fancy, but there's a bit of a backyard with it and a tree for some shade. He grilled us steaks on a small barbecue and we ate outside under the tree.

My dad had the sweater I'd given to him weeks ago on and I also gave him the red scarf I had recently finished knitting. He wrapped that scarf around his neck like it was his most precious possession. Just having him back was the best present I could have imagined.

My mother started packing the day after Christmas. She's going to move in with my dad just as soon as I get my first paycheck and find a room to rent. Uncle Lou is back from Italy and he didn't hesitate for a moment when I asked about the job. I've already worked a few shifts and my hours at The Pews will work in well with my class schedule. Other people have put themselves through school. I can, too.

I hear a knock on the door of the Sisterhood room and I look up.

Lizabett and Becca are both there so I motion for them to come inside.

The Christmas decorations are hanging on both sides of the French door and the air outside is still cold. Both Becca and Lizabett have rosy cheeks. Tonight Uncle Lou will be bringing us our tea.

It doesn't take us long to get everyone settled down to their knitting.

Marilee has finished up her blue scarf and I even saw it around Quinn's neck the other day. Becca finished the turquoise cap she was knitting, but she won't say who she gave it to. I'm guessing it was Joy, since Becca has spent days filling out forms and calling government offices to get Joy the medical care she needs. Lizabett wasn't making a Christmas present so she's still knitting away.

We are all talking about what to do next and are trying to settle on the yarn we want to use next.

"January's a good time of year to begin new projects," I say as I pull the Sisterhood journal off of the bookshelf and set it on the table.

I would keep the Sisterhood journal in my hands forever, but I know that's not fair. It helped me to be able to write my thoughts down when I was troubled. "It's time for someone else to take the journal with them."

Marilee studies me a moment and then nods. "Yes, it's time."

"Becca?" I push the journal in her direction. "You're next if we're going by age."

"I don't know if I'll be able to—" Becca protests and then lets her words die out. "Do you think it would work for me, too?"

"What do you mean?" Marilee asks.

"Well, both of you look so much more content now," Becca says. "I was just wondering if it will make me calmer."

"Not unless you want it to," I assure her.

"I don't know what I want," Becca says bleakly. Knowing her, I can tell that is a statement of despair. Becca always knows what she wants, or at least she used to know.

"Problems?" I ask.

Becca hesitates and then reaches out her arm to pull the Sisterhood journal toward her. "Nothing I can't handle."

I could give Becca a lecture on secrets, but I don't. "If you need us, we'll be there."

Becca nods as she picks the Sisterhood journal up and holds it. "I know."

There's a knock on the door and I look up to see Uncle Lou, Quinn and Randy.

"We're just going to pour your tea and then leave," Quinn says as he puts his head in the door. "We know you're not done talking yet."

"That's right. We're making our own plans in the kitchen," Randy says as he carries in a tray that holds four cups of some tea that Uncle Lou found in Italy and a plate of imported biscotti.

Randy winks at me. "See you when you're finished."

I didn't know Randy would be here tonight so I'm grinning up at him like the lovesick fool that I am. I notice Marilee has a similar look on her face. I think Quinn surprised her as well.

"You girls need to keep up your strength," Uncle Lou says as he sets the cups down in front of each one of us.

When we have our tea, the men leave the room and go back to the counter to sit down.

I happen to glance over at Becca and I see she's looking at Marilee, who's watching Quinn through the glass panes in the French doors. Becca has a funny look of half misery and half longing on her face.

"Why you've got a boyfriend," I blurt out without thinking and I see a flush of color on Becca's face.

"Not really," she says, but her color has already given her away.

"Well," Marilee says, turning from the window and sounding very pleased. "You definitely need to have the journal then."

"And no fair taping all of the pages shut, either," Lizabett says, with a grin. "I've been waiting for this."

"There's nothing to tell," Becca grumbles.

"The road to true love is never smooth," I say. Maybe Becca didn't give the cap she knit to Joy, after all. "There will always be things to say, I guarantee it."

"You're going to have to help me then," Becca says with a sigh.

"We're the Sisterhood," I say softly. "Of course we'll help you."

I look up at Randy and I see he's looking through

the glass panes at me. I am so fortunate. "You all helped me with Randy," I say.

"And me with Quinn," Marilee adds.

"Then I suppose I am next," Becca says, although she doesn't sound a bit happy about it. She does keep a firm hold on the Sisterhood journal, though, and I know she'll carry through. Becca always does what she has to do, whether she wants to do it or not.

After we've finished our Sisterhood meeting, Randy asks me if I'd like to walk down Colorado Boulevard with him before he drives me home. I say yes. There's something about walking down this well-lit street in the evening that makes me think of old classic movies. Most of the shops are open late and soft light shines out from each window. There's a man standing on the corner with his saxophone playing some Delta blues; he's got a hat out for tips and Randy puts in a few dollars. Several of the restaurants have sidewalk seating and the candles on the tables give a golden hue to the night. People are walking up and down the street, talking and laughing.

Randy and I walk all the way down to the bridge that goes over the Arroyo Seco canyon beneath us. It's quieter here. Randy has his arm around me and we look at the lights from the houses on the other side of the canyon.

"There's a house that still has its Christmas lights up," Randy says as he points.

"I still have the lights strung on the balcony at my uncle's house, too. I don't want Christmas to end."

"I know what you mean."

"Of course, I don't turn the lights on even though they're still up," I say. "I wouldn't want you to think I'm one of those Christmas-trees-up-until-Easter people."

"I wouldn't care if you were."

"Oh."

Randy smiles down at me. "If you haven't figured it out by now, pretty much anything you do is okay with me."

And then he kisses me. Which is pretty much okay with me, too.

* * * * *

Dear Reader,

One of the really good things in life is that God has put us all in different packages. Some of us are short, some tall, some conventionally beautiful, some not. We're blondes, brunettes and sometimes even bald.

When I started writing "The Sisterhood of the Dropped Stitches" series, I deliberately created the characters to look different from each other. Particularly when we're teenagers, we're almost all a little self-conscious about the way we look. That's why I wanted one of the characters in the series to be stunningly gorgeous.

Carly is the one I chose to be beautiful. I wanted to show that, even though she looks so together on the outside, on the inside she has the same insecurities that others do. Her friends think she has everything going for her. She lives in an upscale neighborhood in a fantastic house. The guys think she's beautiful. Her clothes are nice and she never has a bad hair day. But, at the end of the day, she sits with her cat and wonders if she's doing something wrong.

I also wanted to tell Carly's story at Christmastime because I wanted to show her comparing herself to a teenage girl, Mary, who was born into very different circumstances thousands of years ago. I've often wondered if Mary worried about anything that today's teenagers worry about. I suspect she did.

This Christmas, I am going to try to understand Mary and Joseph more deeply. I invite you to do the same. I believe we have a lot we can learn from each of them.

I hope you have a Merry Christmas.

Janet Tronstad

QUESTIONS FOR DISCUSSION

1. Have you ever faced a situation like Carly's where you have not provided information and let people believe something that is not true? Do you think it is a lie to deceive people in this manner?

2. When do you think Carly should have told her friends the truth about her family situation? The first day they met? A month later? A year later?

3. Have you ever been in a friendship group like the Sisterhood? Tell us about it.

4. Carly had a hard time trusting men because she didn't think they saw the real Carly. Have you ever felt this way in a situation? What did you do? How would you advise Carly?

5. Carly's mother was ashamed that her daughter had cancer. What are other feelings a parent might have when they find out that their child has cancer?

6. Carly and her parents are also ashamed that they do not support themselves. What do you think about this?

7. Becca felt betrayed because Carly had not been honest with the Sisterhood earlier. Do you think her feelings were justified? Have you ever felt a friend hadn't confided in you when you had confided in them? How did that make you feel?

8. Carly's experience with the nativity drew her closer to God. Have you ever put yourself in the place of Mary and thought about how she would feel? Or have you ever pictured yourself as other characters in the nativity scene? Which ones and why?

9. Carly's mother had a tendency to treat her like a princess. What are the good points to this? What are the bad points? Do you think it made Carly's life easier or harder?

10. Which of the four characters in the Sisterhood would you like to be? Why?

Powerful, engaging stories of romance, adventure and faith set in the past—when life was simpler and faith played a major role in everyday lives.

Turn the page for a sneak preview of HOMESPUN BRIDE by Jillian Hart

There was something about the young woman—something he couldn't put his finger on. He'd hardly glanced at her when he'd hauled her from the family sleigh, but now he took a longer look through the veil of falling snow.

For a moment her silhouette, her size, and her movements all reminded him of Noelle. How about that. Noelle, his frozen heart reminded him with a painful squeeze, had been his first—and only—love.

It couldn't be her, he reasoned, since she was married and probably a mother by now. She'd be safe in town, living snugly in one of the finest houses in the county instead of riding along the country roads in a storm. Still, curiosity nibbled at him, and he plowed through the knee-deep snow. Snow was falling faster now, and yet somehow through the thick downfall his gaze seemed to find her.

She was fragile, a delicate bundle of wool—and snow clung to her hood and scarf and cloak like a shroud, making her tough to see. She'd been just a little bit of a thing when he'd lifted her from the sleigh, and his only thought at the time had been to get both women out of danger. Now something chewed at his memory. He couldn't quite figure out what, but he could feel it in his gut.

The woman was talking on as she unwound her niece's veil. "We were tossed about dreadfully. You're likely bruised and broken from root to stem. I've never been so terrified. All I could do was pray over and over and think of you, my dear." Her words warmed with tenderness. "What a greater nightmare for you."

"We're fine. All's well that ends well," the niece insisted.

Although her voice was muffled by the thick snowfall, his step faltered. There *was* something about her voice, something familiar in the gentle resonance of her alto. Now he could see the top part of her face, due to her loosened scarf. Her eyes—they were a startling, flawless emerald green.

Whoa, there. He'd seen that perfect shade of green before—and long ago. Recognition speared through his midsection, but he already knew she was his Noelle even before the last layer of the scarf fell away from her face.

His Noelle, just as lovely and dear, was now blind and veiled with snow. His first love. The woman he'd spent years and thousands of miles trying to forget. Hard to believe that there she was suddenly right in front of him. He'd heard about the engagement announcement a few years back, and he'd known in returning to live in Angel Falls that he'd have to run into her eventually.

He just didn't figure it would be so soon and like this.

Seeing her again shouldn't make him feel as if he'd been hit in the chest with a cannonball. The shock was wearing off, he realized, the same as when you received a hard blow. First off, you were too stunned to feel it. Then the pain began to settle in, just a hint, and then rushing in until it was unbearable. Yep, that was the word to describe what was happening inside his rib cage. A pain worse than a broken bone beat through him.

Best get the sleigh righted, the horse hitched back up and the women home. But it was all he could to do turn his back as he took his mustang by the bridle. The palomino pinto gave him a snort and shook his head, sending the snow on his golden mane flying.

I know how you feel, Sunny, Thad thought. Judging by the look of things, it would be a long time until they had a chance to get in out of the cold.

He'd do best to ignore the women, especially Noelle, and to get to the work needin' to be done. He gave the sleigh a shove, but the vehicle was wedged against the snow-covered brush banking the river. Not that he'd put a lot of weight on the Lord over much these days, but Thad had to admit it was a close call. Almost eerie how he'd caught them just in time. It did seem providential. Had they gone only a few feet more, gravity would have done the trick and pulled the sleigh straight into the frigid, fast waters of Angel River and plummeted them directly over the tallest falls in the territory.

Thad squeezed his eyes shut. He couldn't stand to think of Noelle tossed into that river, fighting the powerful current along with the ice chunks. There would have been no way to have pulled her from the river in time. Had he been a few minutes slower in coming after them or if Sunny hadn't been so swift, there would have been no way to save her. To fate, to the Lord or to simple chance, he was grateful.

Some tiny measure of tenderness in his chest, like a fire long banked, sputtered to life. His tenderness for her, still there, after so much time and distance. How about that.

Since the black gelding was a tad calmer now that the sound of the train had faded off into the distance, Thad rehitched him to the sleigh but secured the driving reins to his saddle horn. He used the two horses working together to free the sleigh and get it realigned toward the road.

The older woman looked uncertain about getting back into the vehicle. With the way that black gelding of theirs was twitchy and wild-eyed, he didn't blame her. "Don't worry, ma'am, I'll see you two ladies home."

"Th-that would be very good of you, sir. I'm rather shaken up. I've half a mind to walk the entire mile home, except for my dear niece."

Noelle. He wouldn't let his heart react to her. All that mattered was doing right by her—and that was one thing that hadn't changed. He came around to help the aunt into the sleigh and after she was safely seated, turned toward Noelle. Her scarf had slid down to reveal the curve of her face, the slope of her nose and the rosebud smile of her mouth.

What had happened to her? How had she lost her sight? Sadness filled him for her blindness and for what could have been between them, once. He thought about saying something to her, so she would know who he was, but what good would that do? The past was done and over. Only the emptiness of it remained.

"Thank you so much, sir." She turned toward the sound of his step and smiled in his direction. If she, too, wondered who he was, she gave no real hint of it.

He didn't expect her to. Chances were she hardly remembered him, and if she did, she wouldn't think too well of him. She would never know what good wishes he wanted for her as he took her gloved hand. The layers of wool and leather and sheepskin lining between his hand and hers didn't stop that tiny flame of tenderness for her in his chest from growing a notch.

He looked into her eyes, into Noelle's eyes, the

woman he'd loved truly so long ago, knowing she did not recognize him. Could not see him or sense him, even at heart. She smiled at him as if he were the Good Samaritan she thought he was as he helped her settle onto the seat.

Love was an odd thing, he realized as he backed away. Once, their love had been an emotion felt so strong and pure and true that he would have vowed on his very soul that nothing could tarnish nor diminish their bond. But time had done that simply, easily, and they stood now as strangers.

* * * * *